Mango Bob

A Mango Bob and Walker Adventure

by

Bill Myers

www.mangobob.com

Mango Bob

Author's website: www.mangobob.com/
Facebook: www.facebook.com/MangoBob

Chapter 1

I never planned to live in a tent.

It was my attorney's idea. A way to cut costs. To save a little money, to keep a low profile during the legal proceedings.

I'm not a criminal and never needed a lawyer before. I'm just a law-abiding citizen working for a living.

John Everett Walker. That's my name. Everyone who knows me calls me Walker.

People who don't know better sometimes call me Johnny Walker—like the whiskey. Not funny to me. It's either Walker or John.

Walker is preferred.

I'm not a tough guy. Usually don't need to be. At just shy of six feet and still lean from my days in Afghanistan, only a fool would pick a fight with me. Of course, there's no shortage of fools these days.

Back in the mountains of Afghanistan, I carried a gun and looked for trouble. These days I don't.

For the past seven years, I was in the corporate world working my way up the ladder at the Moreco Company, a Boston-based investment firm that makes obscene profits by buying US manufacturing plants, laying off all the workers and moving the plants south of the border.

I worked at one of the plants they bought. The one in Conway, Arkansas where they made hand tools. Mostly wrenches and sockets sold at big box stores.

My job at Moreco was as their computer systems manager. A fancy name for the person responsible for keeping the plant's computers up and running.

It shouldn't have been a difficult job. Except it was.

There were too many people at the plant using the company's computers to surf the web, update their Facebook status, and search for porn. Lots and lots of porn.

I didn't care what they looked at on company time. That wasn't part of my job. What I did care about were all the viruses and malware they were downloading. The kind of things that could spread from computer to computer and bring down the entire network.

That's when they'd call me. Day or night, when the computers went down, it was my job to get them back up and running.

It wasn't my dream job. But at least it was a job. Something to be happy about in the sour state of the economy at the time.

They gave me a small office in the front of the plant. Nothing fancy. A cheap metal desk, several file cabinets, a laser printer, and three computers to monitor the networks.

It could have been a lot worse. They could have put me in a stall out on the plant floor. Near the giant hydraulic presses used to pound steel bars into hand tools.

Not many hand tools are made in the US these days. Most of the plants have moved offshore because making those shiny wrenches and socket sets is a noisy, dirty, and dangerous business.

It starts with rolls of heavy steel bars that are run through stamping presses to turn out tool blanks. The blanks are sent to the furnaces to be heat-treated, followed by an acid soak; then to sand tumblers for polishing. They are then dipped into vats of toxic chromium oxide to make them shiny.

If all goes well, the company ends up with a tool set they

can sell at a big box store for twenty dollars.

But things don't always go well.

Get in the way of one of the carts hauling steel bars, stand too near a stamping press, forget your protective gear near the acid vats and you'll be maimed or killed. I saw it happen more than once. It's never pretty.

They told us office types to stay off the plant floor. It was too dangerous for a casual walk-through. Not the kind of place for someone wearing loafers and a tie to be around.

The manufacturing risks involved along with the toxic chemicals were the excuse given for wanting to move these plants offshore. Management would say there were too many rules, regulations, and safety laws to operate in the US.

Sometimes they were right. The plants were dangerous. But more often than not, the dangers could have been eased by spending more money on safety features.

More about that later.

Like I said, the plant I worked at was in Conway, Arkansas. A small college town bordered by the Arkansas River on the south and the Ozark mountains to the north.

Interstate 40, the thousand-mile artery of non-stop traffic running from the Atlantic Ocean out to California, cuts through the middle of town, making Conway an easy place to get to. Or to escape from.

I'd only been at the plant for three years, although it seemed longer at the time.

Before then, I was the computer systems manager for a Fortune 500 company. The name isn't important. You'd recognize it if I told you.

I was happy there. Good pay, excellent benefits and nice people. I shouldn't have left. But I did, reluctantly.

Moving to Conway was my wife's idea. We'd only been married three months when she told me I needed to quit the job I loved and move to a small town in Arkansas.

Her daddy was a land developer there with deep pockets and lots of empty houses. She wanted to live closer to him. He'd offered her a high-paying job in his company and a new house we could live in for free if we moved there.

I told her I didn't want to go. I was happy where we were. She said I didn't understand. It was either move or she was going to leave me.

Looking back, I should have let her go. I should have said, "Go ahead, I'm staying here."

But I didn't. That's how I ended up in Arkansas—and how I eventually ended up living alone in a tent along the banks of the Arkansas River.

Chapter 2

When you live in Arkansas and work at a plant that makes tools, you drive a pickup truck. Usually a four by four. Not that you need four wheel drive. It doesn't snow that much in central Arkansas. But the locals believe there's no sense in having a truck if it isn't a 4 x 4. So everyone who can afford it drives one. Including me.

Mine was a Toyota Tacoma double cab, white with a tan interior. I bought it new, and it got me places you'd never expect to get to in a truck.

That's where all this "living in a tent" thing got started.

It was lunchtime at the plant. I was in the parking lot heading to my truck when a stranger, clipboard in hand, approached.

I thought the guy was going to ask me to sign a petition. Or maybe give me a humanitarian of the year award.

I was wrong.

He came up and asked, "You John Everett Walker?"

Since only a few people knew my full name, I figured I was in some kind of legal trouble. I should have ducked out. But I didn't. I gave him the answer he expected.

"Yep, that's me."

He nodded toward my truck. "Nice looking rig. Ever think about selling it?"

I'd been asked about it before. Every guy in town, and a lot of women, wanted my truck, or one like it. When they asked if it were for sale, I always answered the same way. "Nope, plan on keeping it forever."

The man standing in front of me said, "Well, if you decide to sell, give me a call." He smiled and handed me a file folder.

I shouldn't have taken it without asking what was in it, but I did. That was a mistake on my part. As soon as it was in my hands, he said, "You've been served."

I shook my head in disgust. "Served? You come out here and ask about my truck. Then you serve me papers. You like doing this?"

"No, not really. But someone has to. Don't take it personal. I still like your truck. Call me if you want to sell it."

I almost smiled but decided it was probably best to just walk away. I'd been given papers and wanted to find out why.

The process server wasn't through talking. "Wait. I've got something else for you. It's from your wife. She said to give it to you after you were served."

He was holding a white envelope. I took it from him. "Anything else?"

"No, that's it. Sorry it had to be this way."

He walked away with me shaking my head.

Chapter 3

I put the papers in my truck and opened the envelope from my wife. There was a typed page with the following message:

```
Walker,

It was good while it lasted, but now it's
time to go our separate ways.

Please review and let's get this resolved
quickly.

My attorney says we shouldn't contact each
other until this is over. If you call, I
won't answer.

I'm trying to make this as painless as
possible.

You're a good man, and I'm better for
knowing you.

Vicki

---------
```

She was divorcing me.

You'd think I would have been shocked. But, surprisingly, I wasn't. Even before we were married, I was pretty sure it wouldn't last long. She just wasn't the kind of girl who took "till death do us part" seriously.

I probably shouldn't have married her. But in my defense, she was the prettiest thing I'd ever seen and was interested in me. Marriage, even a short one, didn't seem like such a bad deal at the time.

Of course, that was "love is blind" thinking on my part.

It happens to all of us sooner or later.

She'd been out of town on a business trip with her father for a week. At least that's what she had told me. She could have been with someone else. Or with her father and his attorney working on the divorce papers.

It didn't really matter. As far as I was concerned, if she didn't want to be married to me, then she shouldn't be.

My only problem was I didn't have an attorney. I was still sitting in my truck in the parking lot at the plant, thinking about what I should do next. Looking out the window, I found the answer—a huge billboard on the other side of the street advertising "Bobby Poole, Attorney-at-Law."

I figured since he could afford to put up a big sign, he was the guy I should call. I pulled out my cell phone and punched in his number.

He answered on the third ring. Not his secretary. Not someone who took messages or screened his calls. Just him. Bobby Poole himself.

This made me wonder. What kind of billboard lawyer has so much time on his hands that he can answer his own phone? Was I just lucky getting through to him, or was it a sign that maybe I should call someone else?

I figured since I had him on the line I'd go ahead and see if he could help. I could always bail if he sounded off. He asked why was calling and I told him I'd been served. Before I could tell him why, he said, "My schedule's open for the next hour. If you can come over now, I'll take a look."

Apparently he wasn't very busy. I didn't know if that was good or bad. But it worked for me. It was my lunch hour and what better way to spend it than with a lawyer.

His office was about three miles away in the Paradise

Shopping Plaza. A part of town most law-abiding people tended to avoid. It was, as they say, on the wrong side of the tracks.

When I arrived, it was clear that Paradise had seen better days. There were boarded-up storefronts, empty beer cans, broken glass, and abandoned cars in the parking lot. Not the kind of place you'd want to take a date.

Bobby Poole's law office was sandwiched between a bail bondsman and a pawn shop. Both had signs saying, "Remove mask and leave guns outside before entering."

Luckily I'd left my mask and gun at home.

That's a joke. I didn't own a mask at the time. My gun was safely locked up at home.

Chapter 4

According to his billboard, Bobby Poole wants to be known as "Bobby the Bulldog".

He's the guy guilty people call when they get caught. I found out later he's the "fixer" local drug dealers and gang bangers go to when they get arrested. Using every trick in the book, some legal, some not, he can usually get them out of jail.

The local cops pretty much hate his guts. None of this was my problem. Yet.

When I opened the door to the Poole law office, a small bell announced my arrival. My first impression was not good. A receptionist desk with no receptionist. A row of beat-up plastic chairs against the wall. Thin brown carpet with a permanent crease leading to a room in the back. The place reminded me of the DMV without the charm. It smelled like the inside of a down-and-out casino.

My office back at the plant was nicer. Not as big but it definitely smelled better. Thinking about it reminded me I wouldn't have it or a job much longer. Corporate management had made that clear. The plant was being moved south of the border. We weren't told where. But they did tell us we weren't invited to the party.

No one was happy about losing their job. Including me.

I'd be unemployed in two weeks. The wife knew and it was probably why she filed instead of waiting. If she got the divorce, she wouldn't have to worry about supporting me while I played house husband.

My thoughts were interrupted when a short, balding man

stuck his head out of the back room.

"You the one just called about getting served?"

"Yeah, that's me."

He walked over, stuck out his hand and said, "Bobby Poole at your service."

I smiled. "I'm Walker. So how does this work? What do you charge?"

I didn't know if asking about his fee was the best way to start out, but knowing how much it was going to cost was a good way to break the ice.

He answered quickly. "First twenty minutes is free. After that, it's two hundred an hour. Pay by credit card or cash. No checks."

I nodded. "So if it drags out, it could get expensive, right?"

I was about to be unemployed and didn't want to give whatever money the wife left me with to an attorney. I didn't tell him that, but I was worried I might have to. I waited to see what he'd say. His answer didn't disappoint.

"Yeah, it could get expensive. It just depends on what we're dealing with. Could be just a few hundred dollars. Could be a lot more. I'll have a better idea after I see the papers."

He pointed to the packet I was holding. "That them?"

"Yeah. Got served this morning. Out in the parking lot where I work."

He nodded. "Happens all the time. Let me see what you got."

I handed him the pages.

He flipped through the pages, then said, "Good news. You haven't murdered anyone, aren't on America's most wanted list, and haven't sold crack to an undercover cop."

14

He seemed relieved. Maybe that was the kind of cases he normally dealt with. Murderers, drug dealers, the like.

"Your wife wants a divorce. Let me make a call, get the details."

He picked up his phone, punched in a number and said, "Sally, this is Bobby Poole. Is Howard in? This is about the Walker divorce."

He gave me a thumbs up.

After a few seconds of silence, he said, "Howard, have you got a minute to go over the Walker thing?"

I couldn't hear both sides of the conversation, but I got the gist of it.

"Yeah, I'm working with the husband."

"Do they have kids?"

"Any property to divide up?"

"Any bills?"

"Is she asking for alimony?"

He paused again, gave me another thumbs up and smiled.

The call continued.

"No kidding?"

"She want anything else?"

"Yeah, that's pretty sweet. I'll talk to the husband and get back to you."

He ended the call and turned to me. "Here's the deal. Your wife wants a divorce. She doesn't want alimony. She just wants out quickly.

"You don't have any kids, don't own a home, and don't have any debt or any major assets to speak of. It'll be an uncontested, no assets, no kids kind of divorce. The best kind.

15

"She keeps her car, her clothes, and everything in the house. You keep your truck, all your personal belongings and half the money in your bank account.

"According to her attorney, your share will be about forty-three thousand. She's giving up all claims to your current and future earnings. You'll do the same for her.

"All you have to do is sign the papers and it'll be over."

He paused, waiting for me to say something. When I didn't, he continued. "You're getting out easy. Most divorces don't go this way. They drag on for months. The husband and wife fight over every detail. The lawyers get rich billing by the hour. It's expensive and, in the end, no one is happy, except the accountants.

"But not this time. Everything is simple. It's like a gift."

"A gift?"

"Yeah, a gift. She's doing you a favor. A big one. No demands. No alimony. No troubles. I wish my ex-wife had done the same thing.

"If it were me, I'd sign the papers today. I wouldn't give her time to change her mind."

The way Bobby was telling it you'd think I'd won the lottery.

I was still thinking about it when he said, "Here's the deal. If you agree to the terms, I can take care of everything this afternoon. Your wife has already signed her part; all you need to do is countersign.

"As soon as you do, I'll file with the court. Thirty days later, you're a free man. My fee will be five hundred dollars. But only if we do it today.

"I don't want to pressure you, but the sooner you sign and file, the sooner you lock in this sweetheart of a deal. Wait too long and it could get messy and expensive."

He was in a hurry. But that was his job. Get deals done quickly and move on to another client.

"If you say the word, I'll make the call and we can wrap this up."

He waited for my reply.

I know you're supposed to take your time and think these things through. Maybe see a marriage counselor and try to reconcile.

But I knew the marriage was over. We'd grown apart. She wanted out. It happens.

I was okay with it. I just wished she'd told me herself instead of going through her lawyer. Maybe that's the way her daddy wanted it. I got the feeling he never thought I was good enough for his daughter.

He could have been right.

Chapter 5

There wasn't really much to think about.

If she wanted out, there was no reason for me to stick around. There was nothing to gain from it. All I had to do was sign the papers. She knew me well enough that I wouldn't hold her up. If she wanted out, she was going to get her way.

She always did.

Bobby didn't have to wait long for my answer. "Let's do it. No need to drag this thing out."

"Good call. You'll be glad you did it this way. A clean break with no mess. I can get everything taken care of today.

"Before I file the papers you'll need a new mailing address. You can't use the same one your wife uses. You don't want your mail going to her. You have a P.O. box she doesn't know about?"

"No. All my mail goes to my home address."

"That'll have to change. You need a new address today. I can't fill out the forms until you get one."

It made sense. I didn't need my side of the divorce papers going to the same address my wife's mail went to.

"I guess I need to go down to the post office and get a box."

"No, don't do that. It'll take too long. It'll be a lot quicker to go over to Pack n' Ship here in the Plaza. They have mailboxes.

"Go on over there, get one. Then come back here. It shouldn't take more than ten minutes.

"When you get back, we'll get the forms knocked out and

filed before the end of the day."

When I was slow to get up, he pointed to the door. "Do it now. Get a mailbox from Pack n' Ship. Then come back here."

He was taking charge. Telling me what to do and when to do it. Something he was probably used to having to do it with his other clients.

I didn't mind. I was paying for his legal advice. Following his instructions was part of the deal.

When I left his office, he was already on the phone, presumably letting wifey's attorney know I was taking the deal.

On the busted sidewalk outside, I checked to see if my truck was still in the parking lot. At the Paradise Plaza you never knew. A crackhead might have decided to claim it as his own.

It was my lucky day. The truck was still there. The windows were still intact. Nobody was cooking meth in the bed.

Pack n' Ship was four doors down from Bobby's office. A sign on the door said they were open. There was no crime scene tape blocking my way, so I went in. The place was cleaner and smelled better than Bobby's. An older woman was sitting behind the counter watching soaps on a small black-and-white TV.

She looked up at me and frowned. "Yes?"

"I need a mailbox."

Still watching the TV, she said, "No problem. Forty dollars to set it up. Twelve dollars a month after. You can check your mail during office hours. Eight till six. We're closed on Sundays.

"We can forward your mail to any address you give us.

Even prison. Extra forty a month for that."

I was hoping I wouldn't need forwarding to a prison address, but you never know. I smiled and said, "Right now, all I need is a box."

She sighed, turned the volume down on her TV, and stood. She reached under the counter and pulled out a one-page form and said, "Fill this out."

The form had fields for my name, phone number and driver's license. I entered the details and handed it back to her, along with forty dollars in cash.

She took my money. "You want to prepay a few months? Most people do. That way, if they can't come in, we can keep the box open."

I didn't know how long I'd need it, but paying for a few months in advance made sense. I paid for six and got a receipt showing the address and the combination needed to get my mail out of the box. I checked to make sure it worked. It did.

With my new address in hand, I headed back to Bobby's office. As soon as I opened his door, I saw him quickly reach under his desk. It made me think he had a gun under there. Probably the smart thing to do in his neighborhood. Keep a gun close by.

When he saw it was me, he relaxed his hand.

"Did you get a new address?"

Before I could answer, he said, "Let me see it."

He took the Pack n' Ship receipt, turned on his copy machine and made a copy. It came out looking better than the original. His copier looked expensive and brand new. I guess he needed a good copier more than he needed nice furniture.

He handed me back the original. "Don't lose this. You'll

need it later."

He pointed to a chair in front of his desk. I took it as an invitation to sit. As soon as I sat, he said, "I can file everything this afternoon. While I'm working on the papers, there are a few things you'll want to take care of.

"First, you need to go to your bank and open a new checking account in your name only. Then transfer forty-three thousand dollars from your wife's joint account into your new one.

"Use your Pack n' Ship box number as your home address. Be sure to get a book of temporary checks and at least a thousand in cash.

"While at the bank, apply for a credit card in your name only. Get the card mailed to your Pack n' Ship address, not your home.

"If you have any credit cards shared jointly with your wife, call and cancel them.

"Then go to the Value Self Storage on Third Street and rent a storage unit big enough for all your things.

"Be back here before four this afternoon. Bring cash so you can pay me.

"Any questions?"

I didn't answer right away. Things were happening faster than I thought they would. When I'd gotten up that morning, it never crossed my mind that my life as I knew it would be over before sundown. But, apparently, it would be.

Bobby was waiting for my answer. "Any questions?"

"No, I think I've got it. Bank, credit cards, storage building. Then come back here."

"Good. If you run into any problems, call me. Otherwise, be back by four."

Outside his office, I planned the rest of my day. The first thing I needed to do was to call the plant, let them know I'd be late getting back.

Molly from Human Resources answered my call.

"Molly, this is Walker. Is there anything I need to do there this afternoon?"

"No, not that I know of. Things are pretty slow around here."

"Good. I've got some personal business I need to take care of. Might not be able to get back until late this afternoon."

"No problem. Take the rest of the day off if you want."

"Okay. If I don't get back today, I'll see you tomorrow."

I ended the call.

Molly and I both knew no one would care if I was late getting back. The plant was closing in two weeks. Most of those who had worked there were already gone.

Chapter 6

Following Bobby's instructions, the bank was my first stop. I went in and met with an account manager, a pleasant-looking woman in her mid-thirties. Her name tag said she was Elizabeth Pell. I hadn't spent much time at the bank and I wasn't surprised that I didn't recognize her.

After I explained what I needed, she said, "No problem. I can take care of it."

It took her about twenty minutes to open a new account and transfer my share of funds from the old one into it. She printed up a book of thirty temporary checks with a promise that real ones would be mailed to me within a week.

When she asked if I wanted a new credit card, I said, "Yes. As soon as possible."

I had to fill out two more forms and agree that any card charges would automatically be withdrawn from my new bank account. I didn't have a problem with that. It'd be something else I wouldn't have to worry about.

I was promised the new card would be sent to my Pack N' Ship address and I would have it in a week or two.

When I asked about canceling my old cards, she said she couldn't do it. I'd have to call the customer service number on the back of each card and ask to cancel. She apologized that it had to be done that way, but said that's the way the credit card companies set it up. You had to call to cancel. Probably so they could sell you something else.

Before leaving the bank, I used one of the temporary checks to withdraw a thousand in cash. Since I wouldn't be using my old credit cards after I canceled them, cash would be king.

Back in my truck, I called the customer service number on the back of each of my cards and explained I wanted to cancel. It took a few minutes to convince them I didn't want another card. I just wanted to cancel. They finally agreed to do it.

With the banking and credit cards taken care of, the next thing on my list was to get a storage unit.

The place Bobby had recommended, Value Self Storage, was about two miles from the bank. It took me eight minutes to get there. Traffic was light, but in a rural town like Conway no one was in a hurry to get anywhere.

Value Self Storage was surrounded by an eight-foot tall wall, topped with razor-wire. From the outside, it looked a lot like a prison. At least what I imagined a prison would look like from the inside. At Value Self Store, the prison walls were designed to keep the bad guys out, not in.

A small concrete block building outside the gated entrance had a sign saying it was the office.

Inside, a young woman behind the counter was seated at a desk, watching eight security monitors with different views of the storage complex.

Hearing me come in, she looked up and smiled. "Welcome to Value Self Storage. What can I do for you today?"

She looked to be in her early twenties, and judging by the three textbooks on her desk, was probably a student at one of the local colleges. I could have asked her which one, but I didn't. I was on a mission.

"I need a storage unit."

"Great. We have several sizes available. What size do you need?"

Before I could ask about sizes and prices, she handed me a brochure with all the answers.

I didn't have much to store. Just some clothes, a laptop computer, a few boxes of photos and old documents. I chose the smallest unit. A four by six. About the size of a small walk-in closet.

The girl behind the counter smiled and said, "You're in luck. We have three available today. It'll be thirty-six dollars a month. How do you want to pay?"

I started to pull out my wallet thinking I'd pay with a credit card, but remembered I'd just canceled them. So instead, I used one of the temporary checks given to me by Elizabeth back at the bank.

After paying, I was given a security code to get through the gate and a map to my unit. Even though I had nothing to store with me, I decided to take a look. I drove up to the gate, entered the security code, and watched as it slowly rose, giving me access to all the fine things being stored by others.

I checked my unit. It was empty and clean. Ready for me to load it up with my worldly possessions.

I'd taken care of the bank, the credit cards, and the storage unit. Everything on Bobby's list. It was three o'clock and I was an hour ahead of schedule.

Maybe Bobby wouldn't mind if I got back early.

There were more cars in the Paradise lot than when I left. Most were parked near the Lion's Den, a gentleman's club ten doors down from Bobby's office.

The sign outside said the showgirls would be on stage at four. Until then, it was just food and drinks. I figured the cars in the lot belonged to early birds wanting to get a good seat before the show started. There was a chance they could have been there for the food. I'm sure that's what they told their

27

wives. That they were there for the food. Nothing else.

I hadn't eaten but wasn't tempted to try the food at the Lion's Den. A place with dancers on the stage usually isn't too fussy about the expire dates on the food they serve. I decided to skip lunch and head to Bobby's office.

When I pushed open his door, he quickly reached under his desk. Same as before. There was no doubt in my mind he had a gun stashed under there.

When he saw it was me, he relaxed and said, "You're back. Get everything taken care of?"

"Yeah. No problems."

He pointed to the chair in front of his desk and I took a seat. "The courier brought the docs. All you need to do is sign them in front of a notary. We can do that at the bail bonds office. You ready?"

"Yeah, I guess."

He stood. "Follow me."

Outside his office, he stopped to lock the door. A good idea in his neighborhood.

The bail bonds was next door. Going inside, I was impressed. It was clean, didn't have any strange smells, and no one looked like Dog the Bounty Hunter.

A middle-aged black woman behind the counter greeted us with a smile. "Bobby, you back here again? How much bail you need this time?"

He laughed. "Shirley, you're looking good today. Your husband know you dress like that in public?"

She smiled. "You know he does. What have you got for me?"

He pointed at me. "I need you to notarize some papers for Mr. Walker here."

She looked at me and extended her hand. "Driver's license please."

I pulled out my wallet, found my license, and handed it to her.

She looked at it then up at me. "You're Johnny Walker? Like the whiskey?"

I'd heard it before. "Yep, that's me. But most people just call me Walker."

"Okay, Walker. You sign and I'll notarize."

Bobby handed me a stack of papers. Each one had yellow sticky arrows pointing to where I needed to sign. Initial here, sign there.

I went through the stack, signing as required.

After checking each page, Bobby handed the stack to Shirley. She used her notary stamp at the bottom of most of the pages, and when she was done, said, "That'll be twenty-five dollars, cash."

I paid with a twenty and a five. Bobby thanked her and we headed back to his place. He unlocked the door but didn't go in. Instead, he peeked in and looked around. Not seeing anyone inside, he said, "All clear."

I was thinking there was a time when it wasn't "all clear" and he had learned to check first before going in. Maybe that's why he kept a gun under his desk.

Back in his office, he put the notarized papers in a briefcase and said, "I'll file these with the court. In thirty days you'll be a free man."

He handed me a handwritten itemized bill. Three fifty for his services, one fifty for court costs. Five hundred total. Less than I'd expected.

I offered to pay with a temporary check, but he said he

preferred cash. I didn't blame him. The temporary checks didn't look real. I reached into my pocket, counted out five one-hundred-dollar bills, and handed them to him.

I thanked him for his time and stood, planning to leave.

He wasn't through with me. "Don't run off. We're not done just yet. There's one small detail in the divorce papers you may have overlooked.

"According to what you just signed, you've agreed to be out of your wife's home by eight tonight. If you're still there after then, you'll be trespassing. Anything you leave after eight becomes her property."

I knew I'd have to move out sooner or later. The house belonged to her father and there was no way he was going to let me live in it after his daughter divorced me. Still, I had assumed at the very least he'd give me a week or two to get my things out.

I was wrong. He wanted me out immediately.

There was a good chance his attorneys had added that clause without my wife knowing about it. She had always been fair, and it didn't seem like something she'd do. But her father would do it. It would be a way for him to get in the last shot.

I wasn't going to let his childishness upset me. I had signed the papers and it was settled. I was moving out. That night. Before eight.

It wouldn't be much of a problem. I could go over to the house, load my things into my truck, and take them to the storage unit. It'd take less than an hour.

But then what? After I moved out, I'd technically be homeless. With nowhere to go.

Almost all of the few friends I'd made since moving to Conway worked at the plant. Most were fired a month earlier.

Many had left town. The ones who hadn't wouldn't be happy to see me. I was one of the few who still had a job—even if it was just for a few more days.

As an office guy, a lot of plant workers felt I was somehow responsible for the decision to fire everyone and move the plant south, even though I had nothing to do with it.

But I understood. Factory guys and office guys usually didn't hang out together. That meant there were no work friends who could take me in for a few days.

My nearest relative lived twelve hundred miles away. I had no family close by to bunk with and no ex-girlfriends or ex-wives to take me in.

My only option was to check into a motel.

But in Conway even the cheapest rooms went for seventy a night. You'd better be armed if you wanted to stay in one of those places.

Motels with prices starting at one twenty a night were safer. But I wasn't interested in them. My soon-to-be-ex-wife would have told you I'm kind of cheap that way. I wouldn't spend a few extra bucks to get something nice if there was an alternative.

There was nothing wrong with trying to save money, especially when your paycheck was going to be ending in a few days.

I explained my situation to Bobby, hoping he'd know of a place I could stay.

It was a no-go. He said he wasn't in the business of providing accommodations for his clients. He did have a suggestion though. He said I could pitch a tent in the nearby state park and stay there until I found something better.

He was serious.

"It'll be like a vacation. You can stay in the campground for twelve dollars a night. You'll have a great view of the river, a picnic table, and a bathhouse with clean toilets and hot showers. Everything you need."

He made it sound good. But I wasn't so sure.

I'd been camping before. The last time was in Afghanistan and it hadn't been fun. Before then, camping was something I enjoyed. Getting away in the woods for a few days. Being one with nature. With the right gear and nice weather, it wouldn't be bad.

The more I thought about it the more I was convinced it was the best option. Instead of paying almost a hundred a night to stay in a cheap motel, I could camp out at the state park for a lot less. And, quoting Bobby, "It would be like a vacation."

So that was my plan. Set up camp in the state park, down by the river. Just me and my truck. In the woods of Arkansas in the fall. It'd be like a vacation.

Or maybe not.

Chapter 7

That's how it came to be that I was living in a tent. A big blue one from Walmart.

After leaving Bobby's office, I drove home and loaded everything I owned into my truck.

All my clothes, a couple pairs of shoes, my laptop computer, a few books, a box of old documents and photos. And my gun. A stainless steel Smith & Wesson 357 magnum revolver.

I hadn't shot it in years and hoped not to have to shoot it any time soon. But if I did, it'd get the job done.

Packing only took about 30 minutes, which, if you think about it, is pretty depressing. All my worldly possessions took less than a half-hour to pack into just a few boxes.

I had started at five thirty and was done before six. I was out of the house well before the deadline. Knowing that I was gone should have made her father happy. And maybe it did. But I doubted it. Nothing I did ever seemed to make him happy. That was just the way he was.

After leaving what was once my home, my next stop was Value Self Storage.

The security code given to me when I rented the unit got me through the gate. From there, I drove to my closet sized storage locker and started unloading my truck. Ten minutes later, I was done. My worldly possessions didn't fill half the closet-sized space.

Since I still needed to keep up appearances at work, I packed a small bag with my office clothes, clean underwear, socks, and a shaving kit. I put it in the backseat of my truck.

Leaving the storage unit, I headed to the Walmart Super Center on the interstate. In the sporting goods section, I got a Coleman 10' x 8' instant up tent, a sleeping bag, a fluorescent lantern, an air bed, and an ice chest. Everything I figured I needed to start my camping adventure.

In the food section, I grabbed a twelve-pack of bottled water, a box of crackers, and a chicken Caesar salad from the deli. Enough supplies to get me through the night. Or so I thought.

Next stop, Toad Suck Ferry State Park.

Yes, it's a real place. Look it up and you'll find it's just south of Conway on the Arkansas River. An easy eight-mile drive from the Moreco plant where I worked.

During spring and summer, the park stays busy, filled with vacationers, picnickers, and family reunions. But it was late fall when I headed there. The kids were back in school, the water was too cold to swim, the weather unpredictable, and the fish weren't biting.

It was after dark when I arrived. A notice on the gatehouse said, "Choose any unoccupied spot. Pay the ranger in the morning."

As expected, the campground was mostly empty. I drove the camping loops until I found a site on the river, close to the restrooms.

When the campground is busy, you wouldn't want to camp near the bathhouse. Too much foot traffic. But when camping in a tent without a toilet, especially when no one else is in the campground, being near the restroom can work in your favor.

Before pulling into my chosen site, I got out with a flashlight to make sure it was unoccupied and didn't have any issues that would create a problem later on. I didn't want to be sleeping near a drainage ditch or uncovered septic tank.

Fortunately, the site checked out. I didn't see anything that would inconvenience my stay.

Parking my truck on the paved pad near the site, I left the headlights on so I could see to pitch the tent. The one I'd gotten was shock-corded, the kind where, in theory, all you have to do is lay it flat on the ground and pull up from the center and you'd be done.

I found a spot that looked pretty good, made sure there weren't any big rocks or sticks that would cause problem, and spread the tent out. With one hand, I grabbed the center of it and pulled straight up. It quickly expanded to full size, with its shocked corded ribs locking everything in place.

It took less than a minute to set it up. I was impressed. I thought for sure that a tent from Walmart would give me trouble. But it hadn't.

I planned to stay in the tent for a few days so I staked the corners to the ground. I didn't want it blowing away if a storm came up. In the late fall in Arkansas, they can come up quickly.

With the tent secure, I unzipped the door and stepped in. I was surprised by the amount of room inside.

It was tall enough that I could move around without bumping my head. That would make staying in it easier.

I brought in the lantern from Walmart and put it in the center of the floor. When I turned it on, it gave the place a homey feel. Camping in the tent might not be bad after all.

I grabbed the rest of my gear from the truck. The sleeping bag, inflatable bed, the ice chest with the food, and the bag with my clothes.

I set the bed up on the east side of the tent and the ice chest with the food across from it. I knew from experience that keeping the food and bed separate is a must when camping in the woods. You never know what kind of visitors the smell of food might attract.

When all my gear was stowed, I sat on the bed and looked around at my new home. It wasn't exactly what I'd planned when I started the day. But it could have been a lot worse. I could have been sleeping in a flea-invested flop house, paying way too much a night to listen to druggies fight in the rooms next to mine.

I kept reminding myself what Bobby had said. "You're getting off easy. The wife is doing you a favor. Living in a tent will be like a vacation."

Of course, he didn't know what was going to happen next.

Chapter 8

The first two days of tent camping went well. There weren't many other people in the campground and I had the place pretty much to myself. Just me and the snowbirds in their big RVs stopping overnight on their annual trek to the warmer climes of the south.

For them, it was a vacation. For me it wasn't. I still had to get up each morning and go to my office at the plant. I quickly learned that getting ready for work while living in a tent is not as easy as you'd think.

My morning routine was as follows. Get up at sunrise. Put on sweats and running shoes. Run the trail around the park, trying to cover at least five miles. Get back from the run, find the least wrinkled office shirt and pants, grab my shaving gear, and make a trip to the bathhouse, an unheated cinder block building with fairly primitive provisions.

The good news was the bathhouse showers had warm water, the toilets flushed, and there was a mirror to shave by. The bad news was it was an open-air affair. No doors to keep the bugs or occasional amphibians out.

Still, compared to camping in Afghanistan, it was paradise. No one shooting at me, no scorpions, no blowing sand, no hundred-plus temps.

At twelve dollars a night, camping at Toad Suck was a bargain. It was quieter and cleaner than some of the high-priced hotels I'd stayed in. Or course, there was no cable TV and no maid service.

But at twelve bucks a night, I didn't miss it.

The park ranger kept an eye on things during the day, and

other than the occasional raccoon, no one had bothered my tent.

Still, it wasn't what I'd call a vacation. I was living in a tent, sleeping on an air mattress on the ground, and sharing my bathroom duties with strangers. On top of that, I had to get up each morning and go to my office at the plant. There, I'd sit at my desk and wonder how my life had gone so far off the rails.

My degree in computer science from the state university was supposed to open doors and be a path to a high-paying career in the "exciting field of computer management".

For a few years, it had. But then times changed.

With the advent of low-cost home computers, it wasn't long before even eleven-year-old kids could write code and set up computer networks. That's when being a computer expert was no longer a hot commodity.

My job as IT manager had evolved into one of being a babysitter of everything computer-related. I was the one who had to fix things anytime a computer burped. Even if the problem was a direct result of reckless decisions by upper management it was my job to take care of it.

But I didn't complain. At least not to anyone who cared. My job wasn't that bad compared to the others at the plant.

The majority of the six hundred other employees worked out on the factory floor. While I was free to roam most of the day, they were often handcuffed to their stations.

It sounds bad; being handcuffed to a machine. But to prevent injury, machine operators working around eighty-ton stamping presses were required to wear restraining chains— handcuffs—to keep their hands out of harm's way.

It was either use the restraining devices or watch people get maimed. Management was always saying, "Safety is job one." Unfortunately, it really wasn't.

Many of those working on the plant floor used drugs and booze to numb the noise, grime, and monotony of the assembly line. They'd toke up before coming to work, toke up at lunch, and toke up again on their final break.

Others were into alcohol.

They'd start the shift with a tall boy. Then sneak another one or two at first break and another two for lunch. At the end of the day they'd pop a cold one before they left the parking lot.

No matter how they did it, the goal was to numb themselves from life on the plant floor.

Everybody wanted to be somewhere else. It didn't matter where as long as it was far away from the ear-numbing stamping presses and the stale oil-filled air.

I was a dreamer. I wanted to live on a beach in Florida. Maybe get paid to arrange beach umbrellas for a fancy hotel or get a job serving rum-flavored drinks to college girls at a waterfront bar.

Almost anything had to be better than being stuck in a cubicle all day babysitting racks of servers or being out on the plant floor.

At least that's what we all thought at the time.

But that changed when the announcement came down from corporate. The plant was closing. All the equipment was being shipped south of the border.

Everyone who worked at the plant, including me, was being given the freedom to do something else. Freedom, as in we were being terminated.

It's an interesting word—terminated. Something that would come back to haunt at least one of the corporate managers who made the decision to close the plant.

Chapter 9

So I was living in a tent. By choice. While going through a quickie divorce, as mandated by the soon-to-be-ex-wife.

At the same time, I was working the final two weeks of my corporate job—without any future job prospects. There weren't too many openings for IT managers in the small town of Conway, or for that matter, anywhere close.

Still, I counted myself as one of the lucky ones.

Corporate wanted a few of the office staff to stay around until the last day. These few people were needed to make sure that computers, servers, files and anything else of value was properly packed and shipped to the new plant.

As the IT manager, I was one of the ones tapped to stay until the very end. Just me, Molly from human resources, John Colbert, head of plant security, and Allison James in accounting.

Allison was nearing sixty. She was retiring after the plant closed. She figured no one was going to hire her anyway, so she might as well make the best of it. Her husband still worked in town; they'd get by.

Colbert from security had lined up a job in inventory control at the local Walmart. He was going to make more money there than at the plant and was happy to be changing jobs.

That left Molly and me.

She was about my age, middle thirties, happily married with two young sons. She hadn't started looking for a new job and wasn't sure she was going to.

Her plan was to take a few months off and be a stay-at-home mom while she thought about her future.

When I told her I was living in a tent, she laughed. She knew I could afford better, but she also understood the emotional challenge of going through a divorce and losing a job at the same time.

She said staying in a tent for a week or two might be a good experience. According to her, "Living in it will give you a whole new perspective on life. It might help you discover what really matters."

I didn't know if she believed what she was saying or not, but it sounded like she did. She'd been through some tough times and a divorce herself and she'd survived.

I figured maybe her advice was worth listening to.

She'd also said, "A divorce can mean freedom to make better choices and a chance to reboot your life's direction."

She probably told those who were fired the same thing. "Sure, you're losing your job, but it gives you the freedom to make better choices and a chance to find a new life direction."

Yeah, right. Tell that to the bill collectors knocking on your door.

Still, her line about "freedom and a chance to find a new direction" sounded good to me.

Chapter 10

After seven days of living in a tent, the "it's like a vacation" feeling had faded.

It had become, "I'm living in a tent, sleeping on the ground, no running water, and my only company is the ranger who collects my camping fee each morning."

I hadn't bought anything to cook with. It would have been too much trouble to prepare meals. I'd have to get a stove and pans and utensils and, after using them, clean them, which is hard to do when you don't have water on tap.

It was easier to go into town and get something at a drive-thru. In the mornings, I'd eat at the nearest McDonald's. Hotcakes, sausage and orange juice—breakfast of champions.

After breakfast I'd head to work, where I'd sit in my office, and start the day by reading emails from corporate. At first there were a lot of them. Mostly telling me what needed to be packed and shipped. But as we got closer to the final day of the plant, there were fewer and fewer emails. Usually about documents that needed to be shredded.

Often, I'd spend most of the day doing nothing except walking around inspecting the empty offices to make sure no important files had been missed.

At the end of the day, I'd head to the campground, stopping along the way to pick something up for dinner.

On the Monday of the last week before the plant officially closed, just about everything had been packed up and shipped out. For all practical purposes, our jobs were over. But corporate still wanted us in the building until that Friday, the day we'd receive our final paychecks and the facility would be shuttered.

Molly, Allison, John and I continued to show up for work, even though the building was empty and there was nothing for us to do. We spent most of our time reading newspapers, looking for jobs, or surfing the web. Anything to tamp down the boredom.

On Wednesday, two days before the shutdown, Molly walked into my office. "Walker, something's come up. Corporate has given me a last-minute job. I need your help."

"Sure, whatever you need."

She tapped a sheet of paper she was holding. "Corporate found something here that wasn't on our original inventory list. Apparently one of the officers had planned to buy it, but the deal fell through.

"Since it's still here, corporate says I have twenty-four hours to get it sold and off the books. I'm going to need your help getting it moved."

I nodded, looking forward to any excuse to get away from my desk. "No problem. Show me what it is and where we have to move it."

She headed for the door. "It's outside, in the executive lot."

The plant had a special parking lot for managers, hidden behind eight-foot walls and accessed from the outside via an electronic pass-card gate.

There'd been several instances of plant workers confronting the higher ups in the main parking lot, often wanting to fight to settle a score. To avoid trouble, the executive lot was built, giving managers a way to sneak into the plant without being seen—or assaulted.

Molly and I walked to the empty executive wing and through the back doorway leading to the private parking lot. During the heyday of the plant, it would have been filled with

Mercedes and BMWs and other expensive cars. But on that day, there was only one vehicle.

Molly pointed to it. "There it is. The inventory item I need to move. The Love Bus."

Chapter 11

It wasn't really a bus. It was a motorhome.

But not a big one like those owned by the rich and famous. The one in front of us was the size of a small U haul truck. Basically a Ford passenger van with a streamlined camper box on the back of it.

According to Molly, the official reason for the company to own the Love Bus was so executives could work while traveling to business meetings.

The "unofficial" reason was to provide executives a safe way to travel with secret girlfriends.

Hence the "Love Bus" name.

Molly said the company got the smaller motorhome in front of us because it was easy to drive and park and had plenty of room for extended road trips. Executives wouldn't need to stay in a motel. The bus had a private bedroom and bath in the back.

Most of the time, the Love Bus had been hidden away in the executive lot, just waiting for one of the corporate officers to take it on the road. But shortly after its purchase, managers discovered flying on the corporate jet was a lot easier than driving a motorhome. So it sat out in the lot, mostly unused.

According to Molly, one of the higher-ups had made a deal to buy it, but when it came time to pay up, they couldn't find him. He was no longer with the company and couldn't be reached by phone. The deal fell through.

Corporate still needed to get it off their books and it had to be gone before the plant closed on Friday. The task of selling it had been given to Molly.

She had called three local RV dealers to see if any of them were interested. All told her the same thing; their lots were filled with too many unsold motorhomes. They didn't need another one taking up space, especially one they had to pay cash for.

With just two days left to get it sold, Molly had a plan that involved me.

"So Walker, you're living in a tent. I was thinking the Love Bus would be an upgrade. It'd give you a roof over your head and a home on wheels you could take anywhere."

I wasn't interested. "Molly, I don't need a motorhome."

"Walker, hear me out. The company said I can sell it to you at the fully depreciated price. That means it's a 'once in a lifetime' kind of deal."

I shook my head. "Molly, I don't need or want a motorhome. Find someone older, a retiree who wants to go south for the winter."

She wasn't giving up. "Walker, this would be perfect for you. It'd give you a place to live and freedom to travel while you decide what to do with the rest of your life.

"And best of all, you wouldn't be sleeping in a tent."

Earlier that morning, I'd told her that living in a tent was getting old. We had talked about how with winter just weeks away, I'd soon have to find something better.

Now she'd found it.

But I wasn't so sure.

"Molly, there's no way I can afford it. My only source of income is ending in two days and I can't spend a big part of my savings on a motorhome."

She smiled. "Don't worry about the price. Corporate told

me to get it sold and said they'll let it go for a whole lot less than it's worth. As long as they get the depreciated book value, they'll be happy. If it sells for more than that, they have to pay taxes on it.

"As far as corporate is concerned, it's less of a hassle to sell it out right, especially if it goes to an employee and they can show it as a termination benefit.

"So don't worry about the price. You'll be able to afford it. Aren't you the least bit curious about what it's like inside?"

I was. I'd never been inside a motorhome before and wondered what the inside of the Love Bus looked like. "Okay, I'll take a look. But I'm not buying it."

She smiled. "I'll get the keys. Be right back."

As I stood in the parking lot waiting for her return, I thought about the Love Bus. From a distance, it looked pretty good. Nice lines, not too big, attractive color scheme.

The paint was slightly faded, the tires a little low, and there was a layer of parking lot grime over the whole rig. But nothing a good cleaning wouldn't take care of.

Still, I was pretty sure it wasn't for me. I had no use for a motorhome.

On the other hand, thinking about the snowbirds I'd seen back in the campground and how they traveled around the country in their RVs, it did sound like a pretty nice way to live.

And, as Molly had pointed out, living in the Love Bus would be a step up from sleeping in a tent.

It'd give me a roof over my head and a place to eat and sleep. The shower and toilet would be a bonus. It could be my own private hideaway. A place where I could relax, watch TV, and use my computer to keep track of the rest of the world.

It might be just the thing I needed.

Chapter 12

Molly handed me a key ring with six keys, all different.

"Which one of these opens the side door?"

She shook her head. "I don't know. You might have to try them all."

I stepped up to the door and tried the largest key. It wouldn't go into the lock. Same with the next three. They didn't fit. But the fourth one did, it went in with no problem.

As I started to unlock the door, Molly stopped me. "Before you go in, you need to know it might be a mess inside. It hasn't been cleaned since the last time it was used."

Opening the door, it was clear she was right. A wave of stale air mixed with the smell of alcohol and dirty laundry rolled over us.

We stepped back—both of us gasping and laughing.

Waving her hands to clear away the odor, she said, "That must have been some party! Let's let it air out for a few minutes."

As we stood outside waiting for fresh air to replace the stale air inside, she asked, "So how's life in the tent?"

We'd already talked about it earlier that morning and she knew how I felt about it. I'd told her it wasn't a long term solution and I needed to find something else.

I had no doubt that's why she brought it up again while we were standing in front of the Love Bus. She wanted to remind me about how I felt about living in a tent.

I told her the same thing I had said earlier. "It was okay at first. But it's not something I want to do for much longer."

She nodded toward the motorhome. "This could be what you need. A real roof over your head."

She pointed to the open door. "You ready to go in?"

I was.

We ventured inside and it did look like there'd been a party. There were empty whiskey bottles on the floor, dirty napkins and food wrappers on the counter, and an overflowing trash bag near the front seat.

It needed to be cleaned, but if you overlooked the party favors, the overall condition was pretty good.

The floor plan was what you'd find in a small one bedroom apartment. A fully equipped kitchen near the door, with a granite counter tops, microwave oven, two-door refrigerator/freezer, stainless steel sink, and solid wood cabinets.

Across from the kitchen, a dinette with seating for four. Further to the back, a private bathroom with toilet, vanity, and shower. Next to the bathroom, a bedroom with a wall-mounted flat-screen TV.

Up front, just behind the driver's compartment, another flat-screen TV, a stereo and a DVD player. Behind the passenger seat, a swivel lounge chair and a wall-mounted desk.

It had all the comforts of home. It was definitely better than my tent.

Molly grinned. "Pretty nice, right?"

"Yeah, a lot nicer than I expected. Who would have thought it had all this? A kitchen, bath, and bedroom? This thing has more room than some of the apartments I've lived in. And it's a lot nicer than most of them."

She nodded. "You're right. It is nice. I definitely could see you living in something like this."

She pointed to the front. "Check out the driver's seat. It's leather. Get behind the wheel; let me see what you look like."

It was an old trick used by car sales people. Get the buyer in the driver's seat. Let them dream about how much fun it would be going down the road.

I knew better, but I took the bait. I settled into the leather seat and got comfortable.

Putting my hands on the steering wheel, it felt like I was king of the road. The gauges were easy to read, the view forward impressively expansive. The side mirrors gave full views to the back and were remotely operated making them easy to adjust.

Above the dash, a small TV screen. Molly said it was a backup monitor so you could see behind you.

She sat down in the passenger seat beside me. "Wonder if it'll start? It's been sitting here for weeks. The batteries might be dead. Give it a try."

I found the key with the Ford logo and put it in the ignition. When I turned it, the motor started right up.

There was no smoke coming out of the exhaust and all the gauges were working. The speedometer showed just over nineteen thousand miles. Low for a seven-year-old vehicle.

Everything looked good and even though I wanted to resist it, I was getting more and more interested in the possibility of owning the Love Bus.

But there was the matter of price. I didn't know if I could afford it. And what would I do with my truck if I were to buy the motorhome?

I'd had the truck for seven years and paid it off long ago. It had served me well, was my pride and joy, and had been my escape vehicle for as long as I could remember.

Selling it, especially after the divorce and losing my job, might be hard to do. But if I wanted to buy the motorhome I might have to bite the bullet and sell the truck. I'd probably need the money.

Even if I sold it, I might not have enough to buy the Love Bus. Molly hadn't told me the price. She had just said it was the deal of a lifetime. Before I got too excited about buying it, I needed to know exactly what she meant.

"Molly, this thing is nice. I can see how it might work for me. But there are two problems.

"First, you haven't told me what it's going to cost me. And second, I'll probably need to sell my truck so I can afford it."

She smiled. "Don't worry about the price or selling your truck. The company really wants the bus gone. If you're interested, I know a way to make it happen so you could be sleeping in it tonight."

I wanted to hear more.

Chapter 13

I had almost convinced myself that I wanted to buy the Love Bus. Owning it would solve some immediate problems. It'd give me a roof over my head and buy me time to decide what I wanted to do next with my life.

Maybe it would be part of the "freedom to make better choices and go in a new direction" that Molly had said was one of the benefits of losing a job.

Or maybe I was just tired of sleeping in a tent and was looking for a way out. Either way, I was interested in hearing Molly's plan.

"Okay, I'll bite. Tell me more."

She smiled. "Here's how it can work. Raymond, my brother-in-law, is looking for a good four-wheel-drive truck. He wants a Tacoma double cab like yours. But he hasn't been able to find a good used one at a decent price.

"Just yesterday, he told me he'd be a cash buyer for the right one. But he can only pay nine five. That's the top of his budget."

I shook my head. "Molly, my truck is worth at least five thousand more than that. No way am I going to let it go at that price."

She was still smiling. "Don't worry. I've got it all figured out.

"According to NADA, the wholesale value of the Love Bus is a little over thirty thousand. But corporate says I can sell it to you for the fully depreciated value of thirteen five. If we could do an even swap, your truck for the motorhome, would you do it?"

I thought about it. My truck was worth around fifteen. The wholesale price for the motorhome was twice that. If I did an even swap, I'd be way ahead. At least on paper.

"Yeah, I'd do it. I'd be a fool not to."

She smiled. "Good. Let's do it then. I'll call my brother-in-law, see if he can come over and look at your truck. Do you have a clear title?"

"I do. It's in the glove box."

"Good. I'll call him. Go clean out your truck before he gets here."

While Molly was calling her brother-in-law, I went back to my office and got on the internet to see what a seven-year-old Winnebago Aspect like the Love Bus would really sell for.

Searching RV Trader, I found ten the same year and model as the Love Bus. The lowest asking price was thirty-two five, and that one had almost a hundred thousand miles on it. Five times more than the Love Bus's nineteen thousand.

Most of the others I found were priced around forty thousand. If I could get the Love Bus for the fifteen my truck was worth, it'd be a great deal. I'd be getting the RV for less than half of the lowest retail price.

It also meant if I bought the Love Bus and it didn't work out, I could probably sell it and make a pretty good profit.

I was liking the idea more and more.

Satisfied that an even trade would be a good deal, I found an empty packing box and headed out to my truck to clean it out. I didn't want Molly's brother-in-law to find my clothes and bathroom necessities in the back seat. He might think I was homeless—which was technically true.

After emptying the truck, I took the box to my office and got back on the internet to learn more about Winnebago

Aspect motorhomes.

On YouTube, I found a video walk-through showing all the features, including one I had overlooked—the wall behind the dinette was really a slide out.

On the video, the salesman pushed a button and the dinette wall moved out, opening up a lot more living space inside. It was an unexpected bonus.

Molly walked into my office and tapped me on the shoulder. "Raymond is out in the parking lot. He wants to see your truck."

I followed her outside to where a man about my age, dressed in business casual, was standing by my Tacoma.

Molly introduced us and we shook hands.

"Nice looking truck. How long have you had it?"

"Seven years. I bought it new."

He nodded, then walked around it. He opened and closed the doors, got on the ground and looked under the frame. He got up and kicked the tires. "Any problems with it?"

"No, none that I know of. I've had all the service done at the dealer. Changed the oil every five thousand miles. Everything's original and works the way it should."

He smiled. "Okay, I'm interested. Let's take it for a drive."

I gave him the keys, slid into the passenger seat, and we headed out.

Before leaving the parking lot, he tested the steering with a figure-eight maneuver followed by a panic stop. The tires chirped as the brakes clamped down.

Satisfied that the truck was safe to drive, we headed out onto I-40.

Merging into traffic, Raymond got the truck up to seventy, set the cruise control, and turned on the air conditioner.

Making sure there was no one around us, he took both hands off the steering wheel to see how well the truck tracked and whether it pulled to either side. It tracked straight, as I knew it would.

Happy with the way it handled on the highway, he took the next exit, drove three miles, turned down a dirt road, and pulled over.

"Okay for me to put it in four-wheel drive?"

"Sure, no problem."

He pressed the 4WD button on the dash, shifted into four low, and we took off down the road.

After five minutes of four-wheeling, he brought the truck to a full stop, took it out of four low, and said, "It drives real good. No rattles. Everything works."

On the way back to the plant Raymond peppered me with questions about the truck. "Any rust, wrecks, or other damage?"

He was asking the kind of things I should have asked Molly about the motorhome.

"No, there's no rust. Hasn't been wrecked. New battery last year. Tires are less than three months old."

He was clearly impressed. "Okay. I'll buy it. With just one condition.

"Molly told me how this was going to work. I get your truck for nine five, and you get the motorhome. But your truck is worth more than I'll be paying, and Molly tells me the motorhome needs a new set of tires.

"So here's the deal.

"I've got a fleet account down at Independent Tire. If you'll take the motorhome down there and ask for Ron Sanders, he'll put six new tires on it and charge them to my account.

"I'll call him and let him know you're coming. He'll have the tires ready and he'll do you right. It won't cost you anything. My treat."

I didn't know what to say other than thanks. Getting new tires for the motorhome at no cost was an unexpected bonus and made parting with my truck easier.

I wondered if Molly had told him to pay for the tires as a way to close the sale. Not that it really mattered, but she was going to a lot of trouble to make the deal work for me.

When we got back to the plant, Raymond parked near the front door and told Molly the truck was exactly what he was looking for. He was a cash buyer.

She looked pleased and turned to me. "So if Raymond buys your truck, you'll buy the Love Bus, right?"

"Yes Molly, I will. I'd be a fool not to."

"Good. Then it's a deal. I've got a bill of sale for each of you to sign in my office. Walker, get the title to your truck."

After getting the title, I followed Raymond and Molly to her office. Her brother-in-law counted out ninety-five one-hundred-dollar bills and handed them to me.

I signed the title and the bill of sale and gave him the keys.

We shook hands and, with a big smile, he said, "I've already called Ron and told him about the tires. They'll be expecting you. Just let them know when you're coming in."

He gave his sister a hug, picked up his paperwork, and said, "Thanks for making this happen."

As he drove off, I looked at Molly and said, "Man, I'm going to miss that truck."

She smiled. "Don't look so sad. You're getting the deal of a lifetime. Sign the paperwork and make it official."

She pointed to the cash Raymond had given me. "Hand it over. Time to pay for the Love Bus."

I gave her the money and she handed me a signed bill of sale and the title for the motorhome.

"Congratulations, you are now the proud owner of the Love Bus. See if you can make it live up to its name."

Chapter 14

We were still in Molly's office talking about me buying the motorhome. "It's your fault. Until this morning, I didn't even know the Love Bus existed. And now I own it. What have you gotten me into?"

She laughed. "Instead of complaining, you should be thanking me. You're going to love it. It's going to change your life. But you're not driving it off this lot until you have it insured. Go to your office and get it covered. While you're doing that, I'll make copies of the title and the bill of sale.

"Print out a proof of insurance card then come back to my office."

I saluted. "Yes ma'am! Will do."

Getting insurance was easy. I went online and searched for "RV insurance." Progressive Insurance was at the top of the list. I went to their site, filled out a form and got a quote that was a lot lower than I expected. I signed up and paid with my new credit card. Just as the bank had promised, the card had arrived four days after I applied.

Per Molly's instructions, I printed out a copy of the proof of insurance and headed back to her office.

When I walked in, she asked, "Did you get it taken care of?"

"Yeah. Through Progressive."

"Good. Now that you've got insurance, take the motorhome to the revenue office. Get it registered and get plates on it.

"Then go over to Independent Tire and get new tires.

"That'll probably take the rest of the afternoon which is

fine since there isn't much going on here. No need to come back just to sit around doing nothing.

"Tomorrow is a big day. Our last day of having a job and payday. Be sure to show up."

I smiled. "Don't worry. I'm not going to miss getting my last check. But I'm not sure I want to leave you here alone in this big empty plant the rest of the afternoon."

She smiled. "Don't worry about me. I'll call corporate and let them know the Love Bus has been sold. That'll make them happy. Then I'll take the rest of the day off."

She pointed to the door. "Get going. You need to get your RV registered and legal before the weekend. I'll see you tomorrow morning. I might even have a little surprise for you."

Chapter 15

Back in the executive parking lot, the Love Bus was waiting. It looked a lot better than it had before. Maybe because it was now mine.

I climbed in, turned the key and the motor started easily.

While it was warming up, I adjusted the outside mirrors and checked to make sure all the drawers and cabinet doors in the back were closed.

Satisfied that everything was secure, I buckled my seat belt, put it in gear, and eased out of the parking lot.

That's when I learned that driving the motorhome was a lot different than driving the Toyota pickup. It was wider, longer, taller, and definitely heavier. It didn't lack power though. The Ford V-10 could really move it down the road.

Stopping was another matter. The brakes worked fine. The pedal felt firm. It just took a lot more room to get it slowed down. Not surprising for a vehicle weighing almost six tons.

It took me about twenty minutes to get to the State Revenue Office. Parking was tight and getting the Love Bus into the lot was a challenge. After circling the lot, I found three empty spaces at the back. I pulled the bus across all three and parked.

Getting the registration and tags was the hassle it always is. I had to go to the front desk, get a number, and wait my turn.

When my number finally came up, I went to the desk of a woman who's name tag identified her as Dawn. When I told her I wanted to register the RV and showed her the title, bill of sale and proof of insurance, she smiled and said, "You're one of the few people I've dealt with today who had everything they needed. This won't take long."

She entered the details into her computer, and asked where to mail the title. I gave her my Pack N' Ship address.

The total with sales tax and title fees came to nine hundred seventy-one dollars. I paid by credit card, again happy the card had arrived on time.

As Dawn handed me the receipt, she said, "Keep the registration and proof of insurance in your vehicle. Put the new plate on before you drive out of our lot."

Outside, glad to be leaving the DMV with everything taken care of, I put the plate on the back of the bus. Before leaving the lot, I called Independent Tire to make sure Raymond had let them know about the tire deal.

Ron answered. "Yeah, he called me. Said you'd be coming in and to put the tires on his fleet account. If you can, come on over now. We've got an empty bay and two guys doing nothing."

The tire store wasn't crowded when I got there. Plenty of room to park. As I pulled into the lot, an older man waved me over to an empty service bay. He lined me up and had me stop before I pulled in.

As soon as I got out, he walked over and introduced himself as Ron. "You Walker? The one Raymond is doing the tire deal with?"

I nodded. "Yeah, that's me."

"Good. We're ready. We've got the tires in stock and can get them on right away. I'll have my guys pull the coach in and get started."

The Winnebago had four tires in the back and two in the front. A total of six Raymond would be paying for.

I wasn't allowed to be inside the RV while they were working on it, so I sat in the waiting room going through a list of things I needed to do before I headed back to the campground.

After forty minutes, Ron came in. "All done. New tires all the way around. We checked the shocks and brakes. They looked good. Still looks new underneath."

He handed me the keys. "You're ready to go. One of the guys will help you back out."

Even though I asked, he wouldn't show me the bill or say how much Raymond was paying for the tires. It had to be over a thousand dollars. I'd have to remember to ask Molly to thank him.

There was a Battery Depot across the street and since it was close, I decided to get the batteries in the Love Bus checked.

I pulled out of the tire lot, waited for traffic to clear, and pulled into Battery Depot. As soon as I killed the motor, a service tech walked over and said, "Nice rig! My wife and I've been dreaming about something like this."

I smiled. "I just got it today and I was thinking I should get the batteries checked."

He nodded. "Probably a good idea. Pop the hood and I'll see what it looks like."

As soon as I got the hood opened. the tech attached two cables to the battery and pressed a button on the device he was holding. "Yep, you need a new one. Probably cost about eighty dollars.

"How about the other two? Want me to check them too?"

I wasn't sure which other two he was talking about, but if they were on the bus, they probably needed to be checked. I decided to act like I knew what he meant.

"Yeah, might as well check them since I'm already here."

He pointed at the side entry door. "They're usually under the steps. If you'll open it, I'll take a look."

He was right. The second step inside the coach door had a removable cover. After unhooking a latch and lifting up the cover, the tech was able to reach and test the two batteries there.

The findings weren't good. "Neither of these will hold a charge. Someone let the water levels get too low. You'll want to replace them. For an RV this size we usually recommend golf cart batteries. They hold a deeper charge.

"Figure around two fifty for both. We have them in stock and can put them in now if you want."

I didn't want to spend the money but sure didn't want to be stuck somewhere with dead batteries. "Sounds good to me. Go ahead and replace them."

After replacing the batteries, the tech started the coach to make sure the charging system was working. It was.

"Everything looks good. Just remember to check the water levels in the batteries once a month. Top off with distilled water when needed."

"Will do. Where do I pay?"

He pointed to the office. I went in and paid with a credit card.

With the tires and batteries taken care of, filling the fuel tank with fresh gas was next on my list. No telling how long the coach had sat with old gas in the tank.

As I started looking for gas stations, I realized I needed to find one with enough room to get the motorhome in without hitting anything.

The smaller stations and convenience stores wouldn't

work. Too tight. Not enough room for an almost thirty-foot RV.

Near the interstate, I found a RaceTrac that looked like it would work. Another motorhome, larger than mine, was already there filling up. If it was good enough for him, it'd work for me.

I pulled into the station and eased up to the pump. The fuel gauge in the Love Bus showed a quarter tank. I figured it would probably take a lot to fill her up.

I wasn't wrong.

The station had a hundred-dollar-per-transaction limit. At four dollars a gallon I only pumped twenty-five into before reaching it.

Inside the coach, the fuel gauge showed half full. The twenty-five I'd pumped didn't come close to filling it.

That probably meant it had a fifty-gallon tank. It'd cost at least two hundred to fill it when empty. I reset the pump and filled the tank. It cost me another seventy five dollars.

Leaving the station, I pulled out into traffic and headed back to Walmart. I'd been stopping there just about every day since moving into the tent.

This time I needed to get supplies to clean up the mess inside the motorhome and food for dinner.

As I pulled in, I noticed two RVs parked on the far side of the lot. Thinking they were where I was supposed to park, I pulled up near them. Not too close but in the general vicinity.

I locked up, went into the store, got my cleaning supplies and food, and headed back to the Love Bus. The other two RVs were still there. It looked like the people inside were watching TV and not in any hurry to go anywhere.

It was getting late, and I didn't want to be driving after

67

dark until I was sure all the lights on the Love Bus worked, so I headed back to the campground.

The office was closed when I got there so I drove to my tent site and pulled onto the parking pad.

I knew I had a big cleaning job ahead of me but was comforted by the thought that I'd be sleeping indoors on a real mattress that night.

Chapter 16

The Love Bus was going to be my home for a while and cleaning up the mess left behind by the people who used it last was my first priority.

I started by clearing out the empty whiskey bottles, beer cans, and food wrappers. This only took a few minutes. Then I used Clorox wipes to wipe the crud off all the kitchen countertops, dinette table, bathroom sink, toilet, and shower.

This gave the coach a "just cleaned" smell. A major improvement.

I wiped down all the cabinets and wood surfaces with furniture wipes and used Armor All on the dash. I didn't have a vacuum cleaner so the carpets would have to wait until another day.

Cleaning the refrigerator and freezer was a lot easier than expected. Both were empty and just needed to be wiped down.

It was starting to get dark and I needed to get my gear out of the tent and moved into the Love Bus. As I headed outside, I noticed an older man and woman standing near my site and talking. When they saw me, they waved and asked, "You need any help?"

I wasn't sure why they had asked, but since I was new to living in a motorhome, I smiled and said, "Maybe. I just got this today. I don't know anything about it. Don't even know how to hook everything up."

The man stepped closer and said, "Your rig is the same model as ours. In fact, it looks just like the one we're in.

"When we walked by, we were wondering why you had

parked it backward—with all the electrical and water connections on the wrong side."

I looked at the RV then back at the couple.

"I'm parked wrong? What do you mean?."

The man offered his hand. "Welcome to the RV lifestyle. I'm Jack, and this is my wife Jean.

"You're going to like having a motorhome, but there are a few things you'll need to know, like how to hook up to shore power.

"If you've got a few minutes, I'd be happy to show you."

I had all the time in the world for someone who wanted to show me what I needed to know about my new home on wheels.

I smiled. "I can use all the help I can get. But only if you have the time."

Jean smiled. "We've got plenty of time. Nothing but. And Jack loves to talk about RVs, don't you, honey?"

"I do. You ready for your first lesson?"

I nodded.

"Okay, the first thing you need to do is learn how to park in your campsite."

He pointed to the back of the parking pad. "See that box sticking up out of the ground back there? That's where the campground hookups are. Electric and water.

"You'll want to park so the utility bay on the backside of your rig is close to that pole. Usually, you just back in when you get to your campsite. Then it's easy to hook up.

"But since you're in the wrong way, you'll need to back out onto the road and pull past your site. Then put it in reverse and back onto the parking pad. Try not to hit anything while you're doing it.

"The first time you do it in a new motorhome can be a challenge. If you want, I can guide you in. But you have to promise not to run over me. Use your mirrors and backup monitor and keep me in sight."

I got into the Love Bus, started it up, and put it in reverse. The little TV screen above the dash came alive and I could see and hear Jack behind me.

I slowly backed out until he said, "That's far enough. Now pull down the road a bit so you can get the right angle to back into the site."

I did as instructed, pulled forward, then hesitated as I checked behind the bus.

From behind, Jack called out, "Just back in slowly. If you lose sight of either side, stop. If you think you are going to hit something, stop. Keep checking your mirrors and your backup monitor. They'll give you a clear view of what's behind you."

I slowly backed in, trying to center the paved area of the parking pad in the backup monitor while checking both side mirrors to make sure I wasn't going to hit anything.

As I backed, I could hear Jack saying, "Good, you're doing fine. Keep coming."

Finally, he held up his hand and said, "That's far enough. Put it in park and set the brake."

After killing the motor, I got out to see the results of my first campsite parking job.

The coach was straight on the pad and I had at least four feet of clearance on each side.

Jack walked up and said, "Not bad for a first-timer. Now, let me show you how to connect to shore power. You'll need your keys for this part."

I went back to the coach, got the keys from the ignition and went to where Jack was standing and showed them to him.

He nodded. "You'll always want to have your keys with you when you leave the coach. The doors will sometimes lock by themselves after you get out. If they do and you don't have your keys, you won't be getting back in.

"After you get locked out a few times, you'll learn to keep the keys with you."

He pointed to a small door at the back of the driver's side. "That's your utility compartment. You'll find your water, electric, and sewer connections in there. One of your keys will unlock the compartment.

"Go ahead and give it a try."

After I unlocked it, he pointed to just above the door panel. "See that chrome hook? It's a latch to hold the door open."

I gave it a try and it worked.

"Now that you've got both hands free, reach inside and get the power cable. It's the heavy black one."

I grabbed the cable and looked back for further instructions.

"Push the three-pronged plug through the opening at the bottom of the compartment. Then pull out enough cable to reach the electrical box over here."

He was pointing to a pole at the rear of the campsite that had a metal fuse box on the top of it.

"Before you do anything, go to the box and flip the thirty-amp breaker to 'Off'. Then plug in your power cable and flip the breaker back on."

I followed his instructions, and after getting the cable

plugged in and the breaker back on, I heard three beeps from inside the motorhome.

Jack smiled. "That's the microwave letting you know everything inside is powered up.

"Next, you'll want to connect to water. Get the end of that white hose and push it through the opening in the compartment floor. Then pull the end of it over to the water spigot."

He was pointing to a metal water pipe coming up out of the ground near the electrical box I had just hooked up to. The pipe had a threaded faucet at the top.

"It's a good idea to spray the faucet with bleach before connecting. You never know who or what may have touched it last. It could have been someone who just dumped their sewer tank and didn't wash their hands or maybe a raccoon or dog looking for a drink.

"Either way, you don't want to contaminate your drinking water."

I nodded. "I'll have to remember to pick up bleach and a sprayer next time I'm at Walmart."

He pointed at the faucet. "Since you don't have bleach, go ahead and connect to it. Just don't drink the water."

I hadn't planned to drink the water coming from the RV's holding tank. After sitting for months, maybe years, it had to be stale. It didn't really matter though. I'd gotten in the habit of carrying bottled water back when I was in Afghanistan. I learned the hard way to never drink water from an unknown source.

Jack was still telling me about my RV. He pointed to a round pipe inside the utility compartment. "That's your dump hose. Some campgrounds have a sewer connection at each site so you can empty your holding tanks. This park doesn't. But they have a dump station near the exit gate."

That was good to know. No telling what was lurking in the holding tanks of the Love Bus. I'd want to dump them soon.

Jack pointed at the compartment. "Now that you've hooked everything up, close and lock the door. You don't want anything getting in there at night."

After locking it up, I wiped my hands on my pants. When I did, he said, "Yep, you can get your hands dirty doing this. That's why it's a good idea to keep rubber gloves and disinfectant-wipes close by. Add those to your shopping list."

"Will do."

He pointed to the driver's door. "If you want, we can go inside and I'll show you how to check the levels and make sure everything is running the way it should."

I was hoping he was going to say that. There were a lot of buttons and switches inside that I knew nothing about. I smiled and said, "That'd be great. I appreciate anything you can show me."

We walked to the front door, Jean staying close behind.

Chapter 17

When we got to the RV's side entry door, Jack hesitated. "You want to go in first, to hide anything I shouldn't see?"

I laughed. "All you're going to see inside is how little I have. Just the few cleaning supplies I picked up at Walmart. It's safe, go on in."

I opened the door. "Ladies first."

Jean went in and Jack followed. I brought up the rear.

Inside, Jean turned to me and said, "Your rig looks just like ours. Even has the same color scheme. It smells like you just cleaned it up."

I beamed. "You're right, I just finished cleaning. Had to. It was a real mess when I picked it up."

"You did a good job. Looks new."

Jack turned and pointed to a rocker switch near the entry door. "That's your coach power switch. If you disconnect from shore power and want to run on batteries, you have to flip the rocker switch to 'On'.

"Usually you'll leave it on when you're using the coach and turn it off when you are going to be away for a few days.

"If you forget to turn it off, it'll eventually drain your batteries. If you're using your fridge, even on propane, you need to have the switch on."

Jean laughed. "Jack learned the hard way. We put the coach in storage for a month and forgot to turn off the power. The next time we wanted to use it, the batteries were so dead we had to replace them.

"Then there was the time we stayed with a friend for a few

days and Jack flipped the power switch off to save the batteries. When we came back five days later, everything in the fridge had gone bad. It was a real mess.

"And speaking of messes, there was the time he was dumping the tanks and somehow the sewer hose popped off after he opened the valve. Sprayed sewage all over him."

Jean was laughing so hard she couldn't continue. Jack started laughing too. "Yeah, it was a real poop storm. But I learned my lesson. Only happened to me once."

He turned to Jean. "Okay if I continue?"

"Yes. If you must."

He turned back to me and pointed to the dinette. "That's your slide room. You can push the button over there and the wall and dinette will slide out, giving you more space inside."

I moved to the wall and started to press the button, but he stopped me. "Don't press it yet. You need to check outside first. Make sure nothing's in the way of the slide. Could be real expensive if you run it into a picnic table or tree."

He was right. It'd be bad if I crashed the wall of the Love Bus before I even moved into it. "I'll go look."

I went outside and checked. There was at least six feet of clearance between the slide room and the nearest tree.

Back inside, I reported my findings. "All clear. Nothing in the way."

"Good. One last tip—the slide won't go out if the parking brake isn't set. Go check it."

I'd set it when I parked, but went up front and pushed the pedal again, just to be sure.

I went back to Jack. "It's set."

He motioned me over to the slide switch. "Here's where it gets fun. Press the 'Extend' button."

I did and, like magic, the wall behind the dinette slowly moved out, taking the dinette with it. After a few seconds, the wall stopped moving and the raised floor under the dinette dropped to match the level of the original coach floor.

"Wow! That's pretty cool! It opens up a lot of space."

Jack nodded. "Yeah, it makes a big difference. Let me show you a few other things you'll want to know about."

Over the course of the next hour he showed me how to power the fridge, water heater, TV, overhead fans, air conditioner and heater. He also showed me how to check the holding tank, battery and propane levels using the display panel near the entry door.

He said, "By pressing the 'Levels' button, you'll see a bar chart showing the condition of tanks and batteries. It's a good idea to check it every few days when you're traveling. When the black or gray tank gets over fifty percent, you'll probably want to dump your tanks. When the propane gets under twenty-five percent, you'll want to fill it. We usually try to keep fresh water around forty percent. There's no need to carry more than that."

He did a quick scan of the interior then looked back at me. "That pretty much covers everything. Any questions?"

I thought for a moment and came up with one. "What do I do in the morning when I get ready to leave?"

"Good question. Before leaving, crank down the TV antenna and retract the slide. Then go outside and disconnect from shore power and unhook from water.

"Stow the power-cord and water hose in the utility bay and close and lock all outside compartments.

"Walk around the coach to make sure the antenna is down, the slide is in, and everything is disconnected. Then come back in, make sure all the cabinets and drawers are closed. You don't want to leave anything out that can move around while you're driving.

"After that, start the motor, pull out of your site, and stop. Go back outside and check to make sure you haven't left anything behind. Then you can drive away."

He saw the look on my face and chuckled. "Once you do it a few times, it'll become second nature."

Jean asked, "You leaving in the morning?"

"No. I've got to go to work. This is my only means of transportation, so I'm driving it to the office. But I'll be back tomorrow night."

"Good. Maybe we can get together again. How long are you planning on staying?"

I hadn't really thought about it. I surprised myself when I said, "Maybe another day. Then I'm thinking about heading to Florida."

"Really? What part?"

"I haven't decided yet. I just thought with winter coming, it might be nicer to spend it in Florida than here."

She nodded. "That's what we've been doing for the past five years. Driving south and spending the winter in a house we rent in Venice.

"We stop here for a day or two to rest, then we're off again.

"We're planning on leaving Saturday morning. If you want, we can get together tomorrow evening and Jack can show you the route we are taking."

"I'd like that. Knowing how to get there might keep me out of trouble."

Jack had kept quiet, but his stomach hadn't. It was growling like a bear. Jean took his hand and said, "Sounds like it's time to feed him. If you're here tomorrow evening, come by and see us."

Jack turned to me. "We're in loop B. You can't miss us. Just look for a motorhome just like yours. Hope to see you tomorrow."

After they left I felt better about my decision to buy the Love Bus. I'd gotten a lesson on how to operate most of the systems and had met my first RV friends.

That night, I slept indoors in a real bed with a solid roof over my head. Being homeless was finally starting to feel like a real vacation.

Chapter 18

My phone chimed, telling me it was time to get up and get ready for my last day at work.

It had been the first night in a long time that I'd slept well. Safe and secure in the RV without having to worry about raccoons or wind or rain. I had a real roof over my head, a flush toilet, and a shower. All the comforts of a real home.

It was a great way to start the day.

I took care of bathroom business followed by a morning run around the park. After getting back to the RV, I showered, dressed, and thought about the things I had to do that day.

First thing I needed to do was to go by Value Self Store and empty out my storage unit. Everything in it would easily fit in the cargo bay of the motorhome. Then go over to Pack n' Ship to check my mail. I wanted to make sure nothing important had come in.

At some point during the day, I had to go back to Walmart to get some of the things Jack had mentioned the night before. Bleach, spray bottle, disinfectant wipes, rubber gloves.

The most important thing was to go to the office and get my final paycheck. I needed to say bye to Molly and see what kind of surprise she might have in store for me.

Knowing her, it was probably a going-away cupcake with a little flag that read, "Live your dreams." Or something along those lines.

I wanted to get on the road, but not before going through Jack's checklist of things to do before leaving the campsite.

I cranked down the TV antenna, brought in the slide

room, unhooked the water and electric, checked and locked all the storage compartments, and secured everything inside.

It only took a few minutes and I was almost ready to go. The last step was to take a quick walk around outside, just to make sure I hadn't forgotten anything.

That's when I saw my big blue tent from Walmart.

I didn't want to leave it behind for someone else to deal with so I packed it up and put it in one of the cargo bays. I'd get rid of it later.

With the tent taken care of, I eased the Love Bus out of the campsite and headed to McDonald's. It was going to be a scrambled egg and orange juice kind of morning.

But there was a problem. I was in the motorhome and getting it into the McDonald's lot wasn't going to be easy. The driveway was narrow, the motorhome was tall and wide, and there was no way it was going to fit into a parking space or go through the drive-through.

Fortunately, there was a shopping mall next door. That early in the morning the parking lot was empty. I parked there, walked over to MickyD's and got my breakfast to go. With a bag of warm food in hand, I headed back to the motorhome.

Inside, as I sat eating at my dining table, I felt a sense of calm that had been missing from my life. I was no longer homeless. I didn't have a job I'd have to worry about. Or an unhappy wife with an ogre of a father.

I had the freedom to go wherever I wanted. I could just start the RV and drive away.

Or I could stay. Either way, I'd be sleeping in my own bed.

After breakfast, I drove over to Value Self Store, emptied my storage unit, and closed my account. From there, I went to Pack n' Ship and checked my mailbox. It was empty. No bills, no legal notices, nothing. Probably a good sign.

Leaving Pack n' Ship, I headed to work.

The wide-open parking lot at the plant was empty except for two cars, Molly's and the security guard's. Allison from accounting had been paid earlier in the week and was long gone from the plant.

With no other cars in the lot, parking the motorhome was easy. I pulled up across three spaces near the front door, got out, locked the doors, and headed into the office.

The security guard greeted me. "Walker, you bought the Love Bus?"

"Yeah, I did. It was Molly's idea. She said it would be better than living in a tent."

"She's right about that. A tent would not be the place to be this winter. But the Love Bus, that's a different story. My wife and I have always dreamed of getting something like it. Maybe someday we will."

We shook hands. "I probably won't be seeing you again. Good luck in whatever you do."

"Same to you."

I walked to my office and wasn't surprised to find it empty. There was nothing in it. Not even my desk or chair. Everything had been cleared out the night before.

With nowhere to sit, I went over to Molly's office.

Hers was the same as mine. Empty except for a folding lawn chair in the center of the room. She was sitting in it, reading a book.

When she saw me, she said, "So you finally made it in. How was your first night in the Love Bus?"

"Better than expected. A soft bed, flush toilet, and a TV. What more could a single guy want?"

She laughed. "From what I remember, a whole lot more. I know about you single guys.

"So what do you think? Is the Love Bus going to work out for you?"

"Yeah, I think it is. It was nice to sleep on a real mattress and have a roof over my head. And get this, I met a retired couple in the park. They have a motorhome that looks exactly like the Love Bus.

"They took me by the hand and showed me how everything works. They even showed me how to park it like a pro.

"So yeah, even though I miss my little truck, I think I'm going to like having a motorhome. Do me a favor and thank Raymond for the deal on the tires. He saved me a lot of money."

Molly nodded. "I'll do that. He called last night and couldn't help but talk about his new truck. He really likes it."

She paused. "Now that you have new tires, what are your plans? Are you going to stay at the park or are you going to hit the road?"

Instead of answering right away, I thought about what Jack and Jean had talked about the night before. About going south for the winter. With the Love Bus, I could do the same. I let Molly know.

"I'm thinking about driving to Florida. Maybe find a small town near the beach, set up camp, and relax for a while."

She smiled. "That sounds nice, especially the part about camping near the beach. If that's what you really want to do, I might be able to help you out. But first you'll want to see these."

She handed me three envelopes.

The first had my monthly paycheck inside. The second had my severance pay—equivalent to one month of my regular salary.

The third and final one had a check for four weeks of accumulated but unused vacation. Together, the three checks added up to just under thirty thousand dollar. A lot more than I was expecting.

I knew I was going to get vacation and termination pay, but I never thought it was going to add up to be so much. I was definitely happy that it did.

My last day at work was off to a good start.

Molly saw the surprised look on my face and asked, "Is there a problem?"

"No, not at all. It's just more than I expected."

"Good. I hope it means you're in a good mood because I want to ask you for a favor. A really big one. You don't have to do it if you don't want to, but at least hear me out."

"Okay, no problem. I'm listening."

She smiled. "My younger sister lives in Florida near the beach. A small town a few miles south of Sarasota.

"We don't get to see each other much, but she did visit us here about six months ago.

"Back then, she was living with a guy who she thought might be Mister Right. He was everything she was looking for. Handsome, funny, and he liked her. She really thought he was the one.

"But there was a problem. Mister Right was allergic to cats and my sister had one. It had been with her for three years.

"Mister Right claimed he was so allergic to the cat he wouldn't be able to stick around. He told my sister she'd have to choose—either the cat had to go or he was leaving."

I was wondering where the story was going and how it was going to involve me.

I started to get a clue when Molly asked, "Are you by any chance allergic to cats?"

Chapter 19

"Cats? You're asking me if I'm allergic to cats?"

"Yeah, that's what I'm asking. Are you? Are you allergic to cats?"

I shook my head. "No, not so far as I know. I've lived with them in the past, didn't have any problems."

She brightened. "Good. That means you could really help me out with this.

"This past summer, when my sister visited, she brought her cat with her. Right before she left, she asked me to take care of it until she found out if her new boyfriend was really Mister Right.

"We already had two dogs and the two kids, and I really didn't want to take on another animal, but my sister has a way of talking me into doing things for her. So we ended up with the cat.

"It's been six months since she left the cat with us and the boyfriend is long gone. Turned out he was allergic to work as much as he was to cats. He was just looking for someone to support him and his loser ways.

"My sister finally wised up and kicked his butt out. Since then, she's been trying to figure out a way to get her cat back.

"I'd love to take it to her, but there's no way I can go to Florida just to deliver her cat. I can't afford the gas money and I've got kids and a husband here to take care of.

"My sister can't come up here either. She has a small business and she can't get away.

"I talked to her two days ago and mentioned you might be driving to Florida in a motorhome. She wondered if you might have room for her cat."

Molly looked up at me hopefully. "Before you say no, let me tell you a little about the cat.

"He's a three-year-old orange tabby named Mango Bob. He's been neutered and is real lovable. He likes people and is used to riding in cars. He's got his own travel cage and if you took him with you, he wouldn't be a problem."

She was talking faster now. "He just needs a litter box, some fresh water, a bowl of dry food, and you'll never know he's there.

"He can keep you company on the trip. Give you someone to talk to. And if you take him with you, my sister says you can park and stay in your RV in the lot behind her business. It has full hookups and is two blocks from the beach. You can live there rent-free."

Molly finally had my attention. A free place to camp in Florida near the beach sounded good. But I kept my mouth shut. I wanted to hear what else she had to say.

She smiled and continued. "My sister said she might even have a job for you. It wouldn't pay much but it'd be on the beach and out on the water and could be fun.

"So what do you think? Will you take Mango Bob to Florida with you? My sister really misses him."

She wanted me to give her an answer right away, but I wasn't going to. I needed to buy time to consider her request. "This cat, Mango Bob. How'd he get the name?"

She looked relieved that instead of me saying, "No, I won't do it," I had asked a question about the cat.

Still smiling, she said, "It's a long story and my sister will be happy to tell you all about it when you get down there. You'll like her. She's single like you. And pretty."

She paused, then asked, "So can Mango Bob hitch a ride in the Love Bus?"

Instead of answering her question, I asked, "So that's your surprise? Asking me to take a cat along with me on my way to Florida? In the Love Bus? Just so I can meet your sister?"

"No, not to just meet my sister. I really want you to take the cat back to her. She misses him and he misses her. You'll be doing a good deed. In return, you'll get a place to camp near the beach for free for at least two months.

"You don't have to do it if you don't want to. But it'd mean a lot to me if you did. Plus, it'd give you a reason to get out of Conway. To go to Florida. To start a new adventure."

She was right. If I agreed to take the cat, it meant I'd be committed to going to the Sunshine State. I'd be leaving my life in Arkansas behind. That wouldn't be such a bad thing.

Besides, I owed Molly big time. She'd pulled some strings so I could get the Love Bus at a great price. But it made me wonder—did she plan it that way all along? Just so I'd take the cat back to her sister?

I'm pretty naive when it comes to women and it was definitely possible, even likely, that Molly had done just that. Created a plan and put things in motion.

Everything sure seemed to have fallen into place nicely—for Molly, her sister and the cat. Maybe even for me.

I figured it didn't really matter if she had planned it. I was the one who ended up with a nice motorhome at a great price, and the freedom to go to Florida. Maybe even a free place to park near the beach once I got there.

The only downside would be the long drive, the cost of gas, and the hassle of traveling with a cat.

She was waiting for my answer, but I wasn't going to give her one right away. I had to think it over.

"I'm going out to the motorhome. I'll be back in a few minutes and let you know one way or the other."

Her smile disappeared. "Okay, but don't just drive off and leave me hanging. I know this is a big ask. You can say no if you want to. But it would be great if you'd say yes."

I smiled. "Don't worry; I'll be back in a few minutes. I'll let you know then."

Chapter 20

I'd only had the Love Bus one day and already liked the idea of having my own private sanctuary. Just by stepping inside and closing the door behind me, I could get away from the rest of the world.

But how would that change if I had a stranger traveling with me—especially a four-legged one that pooped in a litter box?

Where would I keep him during the trip?

Molly said he had a cage, but if I kept him in it, he'd probably howl nonstop. I didn't want that. It wouldn't be good for the cat or for me.

If I let him run loose while I drove, it might be easier on both of us. I could put his litter box in the shower stall and his water and food bowls on the bathroom floor. He'd be able to get to them whenever he wanted.

With his food and water near the back of the coach, maybe he'd stay close to them, out of my way. Maybe he'd even sleep most of the trip.

If I let him run free, I'd have to be careful going in and out the doors. He might not like traveling in an RV and might want out. Molly and her sister probably wouldn't be too happy with me if the cat escaped somewhere on the road to Florida.

I had to make sure that didn't happen.

On the whole, having a cat traveling with me in the Love Bus with me shouldn't be much of a problem. Even if was, it'd only be for a few days.

I'd made my decision.

I went back to Molly's office and asked, "Do you have an atlas? I'd like to see what part of Florida I'd be going to."

Her face lit up. "You mean you'll do it? You'll take Mango Bob with you?"

She hugged me and said, "I have a road atlas out in my car. I can show you where my sister lives and the way we go when we visit her."

She was obviously very happy about my decision.

She grabbed her things and said, "Walk with me to the front door. I'll give the security guard the go-ahead to lock everything up and we'll get out of here."

A few minutes later, we were in the parking lot standing by her car. She reached under the driver's seat and pulled out a US road atlas, opened to Florida.

She pointed to a spot about halfway down the west coast of Florida, south of Tampa. "My sister lives here. In Englewood. A small fishing village with miles and miles of unspoiled beaches.

"It's about twelve hundred miles from Conway. An easy two-day drive. Interstate most of the way."

She paused as I looked at the map.

It was going to be a long trip. Halfway down Arkansas, through parts of Louisiana, Mississippi, Alabama, and almost all the way through Florida.

A long way to go for my first trip in the RV. But it was too late to back out. And anyway, I was doing a good deed. A favor for a friend.

In return, I'd have a place to park the motorhome and live rent-free close to the beach.

I may have mentioned I like free. The promise of free rent near the beach was a magnet pulling me in that direction.

The alternative? Don't take the cat. Don't go anywhere. Stay in Arkansas and do nothing.

That was the easy way out. But not necessarily the best option.

Going to Florida would mean adventure, warm weather, new people, freedom, and a new beginning.

"You say it only takes two days to get there?"

"That's all it took the last time we went. We left Conway at daybreak, spent the night near Mobile, and were in Englewood late afternoon the next day.

"It might take you a little longer in the Love Bus. But it'll be worth it. My sister Sarah will be so excited to get Mango Bob back. You'll be her knight in shining armor for bringing him back to her."

She took a breath. "When are you planning on leaving?"

I hadn't really thought about it, but I answered anyway.

"Maybe tomorrow morning. I think it might be a good day to start my trip."

She smiled again. "That's great! I can bring Mango Bob and his things over this evening. That way you won't have to wait for me to bring him over in the morning.

"Will that be okay?"

"Yeah, I guess you can bring him over tonight. I've got some errands to run today and don't know when I'll be getting back to the campground. I'll call you when I get there."

She smiled. "Thanks so much for doing this. I really appreciate it. All I ask is that you don't leave without him."

I promised I wouldn't.

93

Chapter 21

It was settled. I'd agreed to drive the Love Bus twelve hundred miles to Florida and deliver the cat to Molly's sister.

I was leaving the next day and I needed to get things ready for the long drive ahead of me.

After saying my goodbyes to Molly, I went to the bank and deposited the three checks she'd given me. I withdrew fifteen hundred in cash, all twenties, figuring the small bills would be easier to spend and less suspicious than carrying around a wad of hundred-dollar bills.

My plan was to use my credit card to pay for gas and food, and use the cash for just-in-case expenses.

With the banking taken care of, I headed over to Walmart. I pulled up to their gas pumps and topped off the fuel tanks.

After filling up, I went inside and headed to the electronics section where I picked up a large screen Garmin GPS and a US atlas—both would come in handy on the trip down to Florida.

Remembering what I had learned from Jack the night before, I picked up a small bottle of bleach in a spray bottle, and a package of disinfectant wipes. In the food section I stocked up on frozen dinners, peanut butter and jelly, bread, cereal, and juice. Quick and easy food fixings for the trip.

Leaving Walmart, I headed back to the campground where I was hoping to see Jack and Jean again. They'd offered to share advice on the best route to Florida which I now needed. Maybe they could even offer some suggestions on places to camp along the way.

When I reached the park, I was greeted by James, the

ranger I had met two weeks earlier. He smiled and said, "I see you're back with us tonight. Where's your truck?"

"Sold it. Got this instead. Beats camping in a tent."

"I bet it does. Unfortunately, the daily camping fee for motorhomes is eighteen dollars."

"No problem. Still a bargain."

"So how many nights you staying?"

"Just tonight. I'm leaving for Florida in the morning."

"I hate to see you go, but the weather in Florida is sure going to be better than what we'll see here the next couple of months.

"Since you're only staying one night, I'm not going to put you in a river-front site. Those are for our long-term guests."

Checking his available site list, he found a vacancy and put me in section D, site eleven. One of the wooded sites. No river views but a bit more private.

He showed me how to get there, told me to be safe, and said to come back to the office if there were any problems. Then he said, "We had some excitement last night. Someone tried to break into one of the motorhomes in the campground.

"It's the first time it's happened. Never had anything like it before.

"The police are still here. Don't be surprised if they ask if you saw anything suspicious last night."

I'd been in the park two weeks, and the only suspicious things I'd seen were the raccoons who tried to steal food scraps at night.

I paid and headed to my campsite, being careful to stay below the posted speed limit of eleven miles per hour.

As I drove, I looked for a motorhome that looked like

mine. The one that Jack and Jean were in. I wanted to talk with them again before taking off to Florida.

Luck wasn't with me. I reached my new campsite without seeing their rig. I'd have to go looking for it later.

Remembering what I had learned the night before, I carefully backed onto the paved pad at my site, close enough to the utility pole so I could hook up to shore power.

After parking, I connected the thirty-amp electrical cable and water hose just as Jack had shown me.

Before going back inside, I checked to make sure there was plenty of room for the slide to go out. No trees or tables in the way. Inside, I set the parking brake, pressed the 'Extend' button, and watched as the slide room opened up more space.

The instructions Jack had given me paid off. I was quickly becoming an old hand at setting up camp.

I put the food and other supplies I'd gotten from Walmart away, but kept the GPS and atlas out to help route my trip.

Before trying to figure out the best way to get to Florida on my own, I wanted to find Jack and Jean to see what advice they could offer.

I was surprised at what I was about to learn from them.

Chapter 22

Toad Suck Ferry State Park has fifty-three campsites spread out over four loops. Three of the loops are on the river; the fourth is in the woods.

I had already checked all the sites in the wooded loop when I drove in and didn't see Jack and Jean's rig. I decided to check the river loops to see if they were camped there.

On my way around the other loops I walked by several motorhomes. Some were the larger Class A's, but most were the smaller Class B's and C's like mine.

Most of the larger ones were pulling a tow vehicle, usually a small car or jeep. Most of the smaller RVs weren't towing anything. Many had bicycles strapped to the back.

It made sense. The big buses would be hard to drive in crowded cities; having a tow vehicle would provide a way to get around after setting up camp.

On the smaller Class B's and C's, you really didn't need a tow vehicle. They were small enough to drive and park just about anywhere. Having a bike meant you could easily get around in the campground or pedal to nearby stores without needing to drive the motorhome.

I might need to add a bike to my shopping list if I was going to stick with the house-on-wheels lifestyle.

Having no luck finding Jack's rig on river loop A, I walked through loop B and eventually found a Winnebago Aspect that looked exactly like the Love Bus. There was no question it was the one I was looking for. Jack was outside checking the air in his tires.

I walked over to him. "You getting ready to go?"

He looked up. "Yeah, we're leaving in the morning. Glad to see you're still here. We were afraid we'd missed you."

"I'm glad you didn't. I'm leaving in the morning too. I wanted to get your advice on a good route to Florida. And maybe some suggestions on where to stay on the way down."

Jack put the air gauge in his back pocket. "Happy to help. But did you hear about the break-in last night?"

"Yeah, the ranger told me about it when I came in."

He nodded. "Did he tell you it was our coach they tried to break into?"

"No, he didn't mention that. What happened?"

He shook his head in disgust.

"It was around one in the morning. We were both sleeping, and I had to get up to pee. On the way to the bathroom, I heard a noise. It sounded like something was trying to get into one of the basement compartments.

"I thought it was a raccoon. We've seen a lot of them around here. I didn't want to wake Jean by yelling at it, so I kept quiet. It bothered me that it might be tearing up the RV, so I went to the window, hoping I could scare it away quietly. When I looked out, I was surprised to see a man down on his knees trying to get something out of the utility compartment.

"I yelled at the man, then ran to the door to see if I could catch him. I was barefoot and wearing just my boxers; it didn't matter, I was going to go after him. But by the time I got the door open, he was long gone.

"Jean was awake by then and asked what was going on. When I told her someone was trying to break into our RV, she didn't believe me. She said I must have dreamed it.

"I was pretty sure it wasn't a dream, but I had been in a deep sleep, and it was possible. I went outside to check and sure enough, I could see that someone had jimmied the lock on our utility compartment and left it open when I ran them off.

"It wasn't a dream. Someone had tried to get into one of our storage bays."

I was stunned. The only people I knew in the campground and they were the ones who had been broken into.

"Really? Someone tried to get into your rig while you were sleeping? Did they get anything? Any idea what they wanted?"

He shook his head. "There's nothing in the utility bay to steal except the thirty-amp power cord and sewer hose.

"I can't think of any reason the guy would risk getting caught for either of them. Anyone who knows anything about motorhomes wouldn't look in the utility bay for something to steal. They'd look in the other compartments where luggage might be stored or they'd try to get inside when the owners were away.

"What's strange about this is no other motorhomes were targeted. Just ours. The guy didn't try to get into any of the unlocked cars at the other sites or inside the flimsy tents or the more expensive motorhomes.

"He chose ours. Like he had a special reason to target it.

"I guess it could have been a prank—but why bother? Why go to the trouble of trying to break into the sewer compartment of a motorhome with people sleeping inside? It just doesn't make sense.

"When I looked out the window, the guy was rummaging around in there like he was looking for something specific.

"He even peeled back one of the metal panels on the inside of the compartment. No telling what he'd have done if I hadn't seen him. He could have really messed things up.

"Jean is pretty upset. Not scared, just upset that someone would damage her home for reasons we can't figure out.

"In any case, we're leaving tomorrow morning. Not because of the break-in. We'd already planned to leave then. The only change is we're camping at Walmart tonight instead of staying here in the campground.

"That'll make it easier for us to get an early start. And Jean won't worry so much about the thief coming back.

"Right now I'm checking all our systems. Making sure our visitor last night didn't mess with anything else. After everything checks out, we'll head over to the Walmart parking lot. We'll spend the night there with the other boon-dockers.

"Tomorrow morning, we'll get up at daybreak and head to Florida."

I couldn't believe what I was hearing. Someone had tried to break into a motorhome knowing there were people sleeping inside. How crazy was that?

"You're spending the night at Walmart? How does that work?"

Jack had a quick answer. "It's called boondocking. Camping without hookups. A lot of Walmart stores allow RVers to park overnight in their lots. Mostly the super centers close to the interstates. A few cities don't allow it, so you have to check with the store to make sure it's okay. But usually, you can stay overnight as long as you don't block the delivery trucks or cause problems for other customers.

"Walmart's smart to do this. It gives RVers a place to rest for the night and most will go into the store and stock up on food and other supplies.

"We usually stay in a campground if we're going to be in a place for more than a day, but when we're trying to cover a lot of miles in a short period of time, we'll drive until dark then find a Walmart parking lot.

"That's what we'll be doing tonight."

I nodded. "So, this boondocking thing, is that why I see motorhomes parked at Walmart?"

"Yeah, that's one reason. Another is that their parking lots are easy to get into. Even if you're not spending the night, it's a convenient place to stop and shop. And gas up."

It made sense. "So you're camping in a Walmart parking lot tonight and heading to Florida tomorrow morning?"

"Yeah, that's our plan. If you like, you're welcome to join us. You can come to Walmart and park close by. If you do, I can show you a few more things about your motorhome."

I had already paid for my site at the State Park and planned to spend the night there, but being around Jack and Jean to learn more about my RV and the best route to Florida was worth leaving the park and moving over to Walmart.

"If you're sure you don't mind, I'd like to go with you over there. When are you planning on leaving?"

"Right before dark. I'm not much on driving after the sun sets, so it'll be around five thirty. Before then, I'm going to do my normal pre-flight check on the motorhome. Tires, oil, things like that. If you want, I'll be happy to help you check yours after I get done here.

"Or, better yet, you can help me check mine. That way you'll see what I do before each trip."

Learning from Jack sounded good to me. I told him anything he could show me would be much appreciated.

In the back of my mind, I was still thinking about why of all the motorhomes and RVs in the campground the thief had singled out his coach.

What could they possibly be looking for?

Later on, I'd find out and it would involve me.

Chapter 23

After Jack told me about the attempted break-in, I decided I needed to make sure I had locked my own motorhome.

I mentioned this and he said, "Go check it right now. Then come back and I'll show you how I get ready for a long trip."

I walked back to the Love Bus and checked. The doors were locked. But one of the exterior compartments wasn't, probably left that way when I moved things from the storage building into the coach that morning.

Fortunately, nothing was missing. I locked the compartments, double-checked the doors, and headed back to Jack's campsite.

He was still outside, bent over the rear tires. He saw me coming and asked, "Everything okay? Any problems?"

"No problems. But one of the compartments was unlocked. I must have forgotten to lock it. I checked and nothing was missing. It's locked now."

"Good. You want to see what I do when I get ready to hit the road?"

"Yeah, I do."

"Okay, let's get started. First thing, I check the pressure in all the tires. Got to get them right or this thing can be hard to drive—especially in the wind.

"If you don't have an air gauge, you'll want to get one. Buy a good one at a truck stop. Those cheap two-dollar gauges from China are worthless.

"Before you check the air, look for the tire pressure sticker on the inside of the driver's door. It'll show how much to put in the front and rear.

"Your tires look new, but you'll still want to check them. A lot of times, tire stores put in too much air and that'll make the RV ride rough and wander all over the road.

"After the tires, I always check underneath the coach to make sure there are no leaks. Then I check the engine oil. These Ford engines are pretty good about not using any between changes, but it's always a good idea to check.

"The washer fluid is another thing that's important. You'll need it to clean the bugs and road grime that builds up on the windshield. Make sure it's full before you leave.

"Inside the coach, you'll want to do a levels check. You'll want to know whether the holding tanks need to be dumped or if you need to add fresh water or get the propane tank filled.

"Mine shows the black and gray tanks are more than half full. There's no point in carrying around all that extra weight on the road. I'll stop and empty them at the dump station up by the front gates when we leave this evening."

He wiped his hands. "That's pretty much it. There's not a lot to do, but you always want to check. We can go do yours now if you want."

I didn't want to impose any more than I already had, but he seemed to enjoy working around the motorhome and I really liked learning from him.

"Yeah Jack, if you don't mind, I'd appreciate your help."

He smiled. "Happy to do it. I'll let Jean know where I'm going; then we can go over there."

He went inside and I waited for his return. When he came back out, he had something in his hand.

"Jean made cookies. She said I had to give you one. Hope

you like chocolate chip."

I smiled. "They're my favorite."

I took the cookie and we headed over to my RV to continue my education.

Chapter 24

On the walk over, Jack talked about the break-in the night before. "We've been camping for more than fifteen years, and this is the first time anything like this has happened. No one's ever tried to break in before. It just doesn't make sense.

"At first I was mad. Now I'm just curious. Why our coach? Why the utility compartment?

"It has Jean on edge. She's not scared, just ready to hit the road. She said the sooner the better.

"When I told her you might be camping with us at Walmart, she said it was a good idea. Better to have someone you know in the camper next to you if you are expecting trouble.

"But really, I'm not expecting trouble, especially at Walmart. They have cameras monitoring the parking lot and security guards inside watching them.

"And a lot of shoppers coming and going. Criminals don't like that many potential witnesses."

When we got to my site, Jack smiled. "Well, look at this. You parked it the right way. Even got it in the middle of the pad. I'm impressed."

"Jack, you're a good teacher. I just did what you showed me last night."

He motioned to the driver's door. "Okay, let's see if your motorhome is ready for the trip. We'll start by checking the tires. Unlock the door."

After I used the remote to unlock it, he opened the door and pointed to a sticker on the door frame that showed the proper air pressures for the front and back tires. "Keep those numbers in mind. If you ever forget them, always check. You don't want to guess and end up over or under-inflated."

He closed the door, went to the front tire, bent down, and unscrewed the valve cap. Using his trucker's air gauge, he checked the pressure.

"Just as I suspected. Over-inflated by twenty pounds."

Using the pointy end of the gauge, he let out ten seconds of air then rechecked the pressure and nodded.

"This one is good. You do the other five and I'll watch."

Following his lead, I checked and adjusted the other five. All were over-inflated. After getting the right pressures, I gave the air gauge back to him.

He took it and said, "Good job. You'll be glad you did that. Now let's check the fluids. Open the hood and grab a paper towel."

Ten minutes later and with Jack's help, I had finished checking everything. He nodded his approval and said, "Looks like she's been regularly maintained. The engine looks clean, fluid levels are good, the belts look fresh. You even have a new battery."

I watched as he looked under the coach.

"You have a small water leak in the back. Probably just need to tighten the winterize valve. An easy fix."

We went to the back and opened the utility compartment. Jack pointed to a white plastic valve. "That's what you turn to empty your fresh water tank. Turn it to the right and see if the leak stops."

I reached in and turned it. After a few seconds, the slow drip under the RV stopped. No more leaks.

Jack leaned in and took a closer look at the utility compartment. He pointed to something inside. "That's different. I don't have that in mine."

He was pointing at a small locked door about the size of a playing card at the back of the compartment. "Not sure what that would be. I've never seen anything like that on any of the motorhomes I've had. I can't think of any reason to have a locking compartment inside the utility bay."

He looked at me. "Any idea what it's for?"

I shook my head. I'd never noticed the locking door, and even if I had, I wouldn't have known it was unusual.

Jack was intrigued. "Somebody added that after the coach left the factory. I guess it could be a safe. But it'd be a strange place to put one. Right next to the sewer connection.

"After you get settled in Florida, you might want to see if any of your keys open that door. No telling what you might find inside."

I nodded. "I'll do that."

I closed and locked the compartment and we headed to the front of the RV. On the way, I mentioned I'd be traveling with a cat.

"A cat? Really?"

"Yeah, I'm taking one with me to Florida.

"You have a cat? I didn't see it inside."

"No, it's not mine. I'm delivering it to a friend of a friend. I've actually never met the friend or the cat."

He chuckled. "Let me guess. A woman talked you into doing this?"

"You're right. It was a woman."

He nodded knowingly. "Women are pretty good at getting their way. Here's some advice. Don't let anything happen to that cat while it's with you.

"If you lose it or it gets hurt, you'll never hear the end of it. Don't use the slide room while the cat's in there with you. If it gets behind the wall when it moves, you're either going to have one seriously pissed off or dead cat on your hands."

I hadn't thought about it. But I could see how it would be a problem if the cat got in the way when the slide room was moving.

"So where's the cat now? Is he here?"

"No, not yet. The woman who talked me into taking him will be bringing him over later this evening."

He grinned. "Make sure you get a litter box. And the right kind of food. Cats can be picky."

Jack pointed to the fuel door. "If you haven't already, top off your tank when you get to Walmart. Your rig will hold fifty gallons. That'll get you well into Mississippi where fuel prices are a lot less."

He wiped his hands. "Looks like you're all set. Anything else I can do for you?"

"Yeah. Call me when you're heading to Walmart." I gave him my number and he punched it into his phone.

"Got it. I've got to get back to Jean. She has a few chores waiting for me. I'll call you around five."

He walked away.

I had two hours to kill before we'd be heading to Walmart. I'd use the time to repack the items I'd moved from the storage building and maybe hang up some clothes in the bedroom closet.

But first I needed to call Molly and let her know the drop-off point was changing.

Chapter 25

She answered on the second ring. "You ready for me to bring the cat over?"

"No, there's been a change of plans. I'm not going to be at the park tonight."

"What! You left without Mango Bob! You promised you'd take him!"

"Molly, calm down. I'm still planning on taking the cat. I'm just not staying at Toad Suck tonight. I'll be camping at Walmart instead."

"Walmart? Why?"

"It's a long story. But I'll be boondocking in the Walmart parking lot tonight."

"Boondocking? What kind of word is that? Never mind. When would be a good time to bring Bob over?"

"Probably after six. I'll call you when I get there."

"Okay, that works for me. It's actually better. It's easier for me to get there than to drive all the way to Toad Suck."

She paused, then said, "One thing I forgot to mention this morning. Harvey Tucker called me yesterday. He's the guy from corporate who pushed the decision to close the Conway plant.

"He was also the last person to use the Love Bus.

"He wanted to know if it had been sold, and, if so, to whom.

"I told him you bought it. He said it had been promised to him and he wanted to know if there was any way he could still buy it. I told him it was too late. The deal was done and the title had been transferred to you.

"He asked if it was still in the executive parking lot. When I told him you had already picked it up, he sounded worried. He said he may have left something in it and wanted to see if it was still there. He wanted to know where you and the Love Bus were.

"I told him you were at Toad Suck for the next few days. I asked if he wanted me to contact you.

"He said not to bother, it wasn't that important.

"This morning, after you picked up your paycheck, he called me at home. He wanted to make sure you were still camping at the park. I told him as far as I knew you were."

"Molly, is Tucker in town? Did he say he was going out to the park to look for me?"

"No, as far as I know he's still in Boston. He didn't mention anything about going to the park. He did want to know the make and model of the Love Bus. Not sure why he'd want to know but I told him anyway. A Winnebago Aspect.

"If he calls back, you want me to tell him you'll be at Walmart tonight?"

"No, tell him I'm already on the road and you're not sure where I'm headed. If he asks, you can give him my email address but not my phone number."

"Okay, no phone number. Got it. Don't you think it's kind of strange for him to be calling and asking so many questions?"

"Yeah, I do. Maybe his girlfriend lost an earring or something. If I find it, I'll let you know. But I'm not going to worry about it."

"Me neither. Be sure to call me when you get to Walmart.

Please don't leave without Mango Bob."

I promised I wouldn't and she ended the call.

Harvey Tucker's sudden interest in the whereabouts of the Love Bus was a bit worrisome.

According to corporate, it had been months since anyone had used it. Why would he wait so long if he was worried about leaving something in it?

Did his sudden interest had something to do with someone trying to break into Jack's motorhome the night before? His rig looked exactly like the Love Bus and could be easily mistaken for it. Maybe the would-be robber mistook his RV for mine.

It was possible but more likely just a coincidence.

Still, it wouldn't hurt that neither Jack nor I would be camping at Toad Suck that night.

Chapter 26

I wasn't going to tell Jack about the phone call from Tucker or his interest in the whereabouts of the Love Bus.

There was no reason to get him riled up about something that probably wasn't in any way related to the break-in.

But Tucker's sudden interesting the Love Bus had me wondering about what he thought he'd left in it. Was it something so valuable he'd risk having someone try to steal it in the dead of night?

Could it have something to do with that secret panel in the utility compartment? Maybe there was something hidden inside worth knowing about. I didn't know if any of the keys given to me would unlock it; I'd have to remember to try them. But not right away. I had other things to take care of.

I needed to get ready to move to the Walmart parking lot. I had to bring the slide in, unhook from campground power and water, stow the power cord and hose, lock all the compartment doors, and wait for Jack's call.

After doing all that, I decided a short nap might be in order. I locked the doors, turned on the overhead fan, went to the back bedroom and stretched out.

Sometime later, my phone chimed with an incoming call from Jack. When I answered, he said, "We're getting ready to leave. If you want to see how to dump your tanks, meet me at the front gate. We're heading there now."

"Give me five minutes. I'll meet you there."

I went outside and did a quick walk-around to make sure I was ready to travel. Compartments locked, slide room in, TV antenna down, electricity and water disconnected. I was good to go.

When I got to the dump station, Jack was waiting. He had the door to his utility compartment open and was wearing long rubber gloves.

I'll spare you the particulars, but dumping the tanks is pretty easy as long as you securely connect one end of the dump hose to the black tank connection in the coach and the other end to the sewer tank in the ground. Only then do you pull the dump handle.

Do it in the right order, things go smoothly.

Miss an important step and you'll end up standing in a puddle of poop.

Jack was an expert and all went well. He dumped his tanks, I dumped mine, and we were on the road to Walmart in less than ten minutes.

Chapter 27

Leaving the state park behind, Jack led the way into town. We were a convoy of two identical-looking motorhomes, both heading in the same direction.

It was obvious by the way he was driving he wasn't in any hurry. He started off slow, kept it below the speed limit, and left plenty of room between his coach and the cars in front of him.

I did the same, making sure not to follow too close to the back end of his RV.

When we got to Walmart, he drove to the far corner of the lot, away from the main entrances and over to where two other RVs were parked. He parked five spaces away from them.

I pulled in beside him, leaving two parking spaces between us.

He got out, came over to my rig, and said, "Let's go talk to the store manager. Usually there's no problem, but I always like to let them know we'll be staying overnight. It's good to get their permission first.

"Once they know we're here, they'll tell us the best place to park and they'll let their security people know we've been approved to stay."

At the service desk inside the store, Jack spoke to an assistant manager. He told her we were traveling in RVs and wanted permission to rest in the parking lot for a few hours.

She listened politely, then said, "No problem. Just park at the far corner of the lot near the trees. That way you won't block our delivery trucks and won't be bothered by traffic.

"If you have leveling jacks, please don't use them and don't put your slides out. We don't want our lot damaged or looking like a campground."

Smiling, she said, "Our store is open twenty-four hours. If you need anything during the night, we'll be here for you."

On our way back to our RVs, Jack pointed to the sky. "This is the best time of year for boondocking. It's not so hot that you need to run your generator and air conditioner and not so cold that you have to run a heater.

"In the heat of the summer, it's usually best to stay at a campground with full hookups so you can run the AC. But tonight, the weather is perfect. All you'll need is to do is run the overhead fan to mask the traffic noise and you'll be good to go."

He paused, then said, "Jean and I plan to leave at daybreak. Our goal is to get just past Mobile before dark.

"It's five hundred miles. If we start at sunrise, we should be able to make it before the sun sets.

"If we get that far, we'll spend the night in the Bass Pro parking lot. It's the first exit beyond the Mobile Bay tunnel."

I nodded. "Do you mind showing me the route you plan to take?"

"No problem."

I pointed to the Love Bus. "I've got maps and a GPS inside. Come on in."

He hesitated. "I'll be over in a few minutes. I want to let Jean know Walmart has given us the okay to stay."

I went to the Love Bus, spread out my maps on the dinette table and waited for Jack.

True to his word, he came over and showed me the route he planned to take.

"I-40 to Little Rock. I-30 to Pine Bluff. 530 South to Highway 65 into Louisiana. Then I-20 to Jackson, Mississippi. Then 49 south to Mobile.

"That's the way we go. If all goes well, we'll get into Vicksburg around noon. From there, it's another two hundred and forty miles to Mobile. If we average sixty, we'll be there before dark.

"We'll stop for fuel in Richland, Mississippi. They always have the lowest prices for gas and it's a good place to fill up.

"The worst part of the drive will be I-20 between Vicksburg and Jackson. That section of the road is built on swampland and the pavement is like a roller coaster. Anything not bolted down in your rig is going to bounce off the walls.

"You'll want to go slow through there. Don't let traffic intimidate you and you'll do fine."

I nodded, trying to keep up with the route numbers and turns. I'd program everything into my GPS later.

He looked up from the map and said, "If we weren't going to be on two-lane farm roads south of Pine Bluff, we could travel together. But motorhomes traveling front to back on a two-lane road can cause problems for drivers that want to get around us. It'd be best if we were a few miles apart.

"If you want, I can call you when we get up in the morning. That way you can get on the road a few minutes after we leave."

He had obviously made the trek to Florida before. His route was planned out with all the turns and best places to stop for gas. Following along behind him, even if I had to stay a few miles back, was the way to go.

"Yeah Jack, I'd like that. If it's okay, I might call you if I run into any problems or get lost."

"Yeah, do that. But don't worry about getting lost. You only have about four turns from here to Mobile. As long as you get on 49 South at Jackson, you'll be on track."

He pointed over his shoulder. "I need to get back to Jean. We're going to eat and get to bed early. It'll be a long day tomorrow."

I thanked him for his guidance and said I hoped to see him again during the trip.

After he left, I got out my GPS and spent a few minutes programming in the route he'd shown me. I was hoping the GPS would keep me from getting lost.

Since Jack planned to reach Mobile the following night, I'd try to do the same. Everything was set. Except for the cat.

I called Molly, but she didn't answer. I left a message.

"Molly, this is Walker. I'm at Walmart. You can bring the cat over whenever you want. I'm parked next to a motorhome that looks exactly like the Love Bus. I'll tie a blue towel around my driver's side mirror so you'll know which is mine.

"If you can't make it or your plans have changed, let me know. I'm leaving at daybreak tomorrow."

I checked my watch. Six p.m. She was probably eating dinner with her husband and kids. Three minutes later, she called back.

"Walker, I got your message. I've just packed Bob into the car. We'll be over there in ten minutes. I'll have my husband and kids with me. We won't be staying long. See you in a few."

Chapter 28

Molly showed up with a car full of kids ten minutes later.

The first thing she said was, "Good to see you're still here. I was afraid you'd change your mind and leave without Mango Bob."

I smiled. "I couldn't leave without the cat. You'd hunt me down if I did."

She nodded. "You're right. I would have."

She walked to the rear of her car, lifted the hatch and handed me two bags. Cat food and litter. With the hatch open, I could hear the cat howling over the noise of the excited kids. I hoped he would stop when we got him in the motorhome.

With water and food bowl in hand, Molly said, "Better get these set up before we bring him over. He's a little nervous with all the kids in the car and might need to use his box soon."

I opened the door to the Love Bus and led the way to the bathroom. "I plan to put the litter box in the shower stall. His food and water bowl over by the sink."

She approved. "I take it you've had a cat before."

"Yeah, a long time ago. I still remember the basics. Food, water, litter box."

"Good, let's go get him."

Back at her car, she handed me a small plastic bag. "These are his toys. Hold on to them until we get him inside."

She reached into the car and came out carrying a large, soft-sided pet carrier with a very pissed-off cat inside.

Growling and hissing.

She attempted a smile. "As you can tell, he's not very happy. He doesn't like being put in the cage, especially with all the kids around.

"When we get him inside, give him a few minutes to settle down. After I leave, unzip the top of his carrier. He'll jump out as soon as he sees an opening. He'll look for a place to hide and stay there for an hour or two. Then he'll start exploring. Keep your doors and windows closed so he doesn't get out.

"After a few hours, he'll calm down and shouldn't be a problem. He normally sleeps all day and patrols at night. As long as there's food in his dish, he'll eat when he's hungry.

"There is this one thing you'll want to know about him. When he needs to use the litter box, he likes to let you know by crying for about five minutes. Usually it happens in the middle of the night.

"Just ignore him when he does. He'll find his box and use it. Any questions?"

"Yeah, does he bite?"

She hesitated before answering. Like she was thinking it over. "Does he bite? No, not really. Just don't mess with him when he doesn't want to be handled. Never try to pet his belly. He doesn't like that. For the most part, just leave him alone. When he wants your attention, he'll let you know."

I had a question that I didn't want to ask but did anyway. "What if he gets car sick?"

She laughed. "Don't worry. If he gets sick, he'll throw up. Then he'll be fine. Really, he's pretty low maintenance. Just make sure he has food and water and a clean litter box and he won't be any trouble.

"If you're only on the road for two days, you won't need to

clean his box. He'll appreciate it if you do, though.

"A couple of things about him. He was born with a stubby tail. It makes him look like a bobcat. He'll act like he's wild, but if you talk to him he'll perk up his pointy ears and look like he understands what you're saying. He might even say something back."

"The plastic bag with his toys has a litter scoop and some catnip. Use the scoop to clean his box. Give him some catnip before you go to bed. It'll settle him down.

"All you really need to worry about is not letting him escape when you go in and out the doors. He'll probably try. If he does get out, you'll never see him again. That'll break my sister's heart.

"Speaking of her, here's a card with her name, phone number, and address. You'll want to call her early the day you're going to get there. She's usually out on the water after eight in the morning and not back until after three in the afternoon.

"If something comes up and you can't reach her, call me. I'll probably be home taking care of the kids until after Christmas. Any questions?"

I thought for a moment and couldn't come up with any. "Sounds like you covered it all. I'll be leaving in the morning, hoping to make Mobile tomorrow night.

"The people parked in the RV next door are the ones I told you about. Jack and Jean. They've been sharing their expertise and showed me the best way to get to Florida. They're really nice.

"Did Harvey Tucker call you again about the Love Bus?"

"No, I haven't heard from him since this morning. If he does call back, I won't tell him where you are or give him your phone number."

She reached out and touched my arm. "Walker, I really appreciate you taking Bob. I hate to see you leave Conway, but I kind of envy you going on this grand adventure.

"Tell my sister I miss her and tell her I said to be nice to you."

She looked over her shoulder toward her car. "I've got to get back. The kids are driving my husband crazy."

She gave me a hug and walked back to her car.

That would be the last time I saw her but not the last time I heard her voice.

Chapter 29

I watched as Molly drove off.

Back inside the Love Bus, Bob was singing. It was not a happy song. He was clearly upset about being confined in his small carry cage.

I wanted to let him out, but not before I went to Walmart and got something to eat for dinner. Maybe a fresh salad from the Subway sandwich shop at the front of the store.

Stepping outside, I locked the door behind me. I didn't want anyone breaking in and stealing Bob. Not that anyone in their right mind would want a howling cat. Including me.

Inside Subway, I ordered a salad to go. There was no need to eat in the store when I had my private dining coach in the parking lot.

As I walked back to the Love Bus, I could hear Bob's loud voice complaining about his situation. He was in a cage and didn't like it. He wanted out. He probably wanted out of the RV as well and would have tried to escape as soon as I opened the door were he not in the cage.

I unlocked and opened the door just a crack to make sure he hadn't clawed his way out of his cage and wasn't waiting for a chance to slip out. Not seeing him nearby. I went in and was relieved to see he was still inside his cat carrier. He wasn't happy, but he was safe.

I put my salad on the dining table and started to eat, but Bob wasn't having it. He upped the volume of his nonstop howling. It was so pitiful sounding that I was sure someone in the parking lot would alert security. Wanting to avoid that, I got up from the table and unzipped the top of his carrier.

Almost immediately, he jumped out and ran for cover, hissing and spitting as he ran.

It would be two hours before I'd see him again.

I ate while going over the route Jack had mapped on my atlas. Arkansas to Louisiana to Mississippi to Alabama. About half interstate with the other half mostly two-lane blacktop.

It looked like it would be a long but fairly easy drive. Assuming nothing went wrong with the motorhome. So far, I'd only driven it thirty-seven miles and almost all of that had been in town at slow speed. I had no way of knowing how it would handle out on the open road.

I was about to find out.

After eating, I dropped the salad container along with the plastic spork into a Walmart shopping bag. I closed all the curtains and rechecked to make sure the doors were locked.

It was still early, but I had a long day of driving ahead and wanted to get some rest. I set the alarm on my phone for six in the morning.

Bob was nowhere to be seen. I figured he was probably hiding behind the couch, trying to keep a low profile until he figured out where he was. At least he had stopped howling. I was thankful for that.

Getting to sleep in the Walmart parking lot wasn't easy. The constant hum of traffic and slamming of car doors, along with the beep of auto alarms, was keeping me awake. At least until I remembered what Jack had said. Turn the overhead fan on low. It'll create white noise that'll help you'll get some sleep.

I followed his advice and soon dozed off.

Chapter 30

In the early morning, long before the sun was up, Mango Bob came alive.

He started with a loud meow followed by six more of the same, all sounding like he wasn't too happy about where he was. His loud cries continued for two minutes, followed by complete silence. I wondered what he was up to. Maybe he'd found a way out.

I started to get up to check on him but stopped when I heard him scratching in his litter box.

He was doing what Molly had said he would do. He was alerting me that he was about to use his box. It was going to be occupied and he didn't want to be disturbed.

He was in it for approximately five minutes. I wasn't sure how long it took him to do his actual business because it sounded like he spent most of the time digging in the litter. Maybe he was trying to dig his way out of the RV. Or maybe he just liked to hide the evidence.

Whatever the reason, he eventually quit and I went back to sleep. No more cries from Bob. At least none that I heard.

My phone chimed me awake at six. It was still dark outside, but the glow from the east suggested the sun would soon be coming up over the horizon.

Pulling back the curtains, I could see the lights in Jack and Jean's motorhome were already on. They were up and getting ready for the road.

I needed to be doing the same.

I rolled out of bed, took care of my bathroom business and after washing up, headed to the kitchen.

For breakfast, I had cereal. Raisin Bran flooded with white grape juice. Breakfast of champions.

Bob heard me eating and came out of hiding. He started sniffing around, acting like he was trying to find the scent of his people. Not finding it, he rubbed his own scent onto every hard surface he could find. Then he began telling me about his night.

He started off with a series of meows, not soft, not loud. More conversational than anything else. It definitely sounded like he was telling me a story.

I listened and when he paused, I said, "Yeah Bob. I know what you mean. It's all strange to me too. But it'll just be two days. Then you'll be back with your Sarah."

He seemed to understand. He meowed softly, then turned and headed back to the bedroom. I was happy to see he had survived the night and hadn't found a way out of the RV.

After breakfast, I put the dishes away and started in on my road trip checklist.

I closed all the drawers and made sure the coach doors were still locked. I opened the curtains on the front windows so I could see to drive. I kept the ones in the back bedroom drawn. I figured keeping it dark back there would be better for the cat. I checked to make sure his litter box was still secure and moved his water and food bowls up against the bathroom vanity to keep them from moving around as we went down the road.

Outside, I heard the sound of Jack's motorhome coming to life. He let the engine warm up for about two minutes, and then, with a toot from his horn, he and Jean drove off.

The plan was for me to give them a twenty-minute head start. Then follow the same route they were taking. I did a quick check inside, made sure everything was ready for the road, and ten minutes later, started the motor.

Like Jack, I let it warm up for two minutes, then after checking my mirrors, I eased out of the Walmart lot and headed for the interstate on-ramp.

Traffic was light that early in the morning. I didn't have any problem getting up on I-40. After merging into the far right lane, I brought the motorhome up to speed, set the cruise control to sixty-five, and settled in for the long drive ahead.

Chapter 31

It took me about an hour to get from Conway to the other side of Little Rock. Then another ninety minutes to get to Pine Bluff where I left the interstate behind. I was impressed with how well the motorhome had handled and how easy it was to drive. At least for that part of the trip.

The next hundred and forty miles would be on narrow rural roads and it might be a different story. Jack had said I'd be driving through the south delta of Arkansas and to expect to see tractors and harvesters on the road. He said they always had the right of way. Give them plenty of room, and only pass when it was safe.

That was my plan. Give everyone plenty of room and stay safe.

When I got to Lake Village, the last town of any size before heading into Louisiana, I pulled into an empty parking lot. The sign above a vacant store said it used to be a Piggly Wiggly.

I'd been driving for almost four hours, making good time. There was no need to kill myself by spending too many hours behind the wheel without a break. I needed to get out and stretch.

I checked on Bob. He was in the back, asleep on the bed. He didn't show any sign that he knew I was up and about. That was good. It meant I might be able to get out the door, take a walk, and get back in without him escaping.

I snuck out the coach side door, locked it and walked around the RV to make sure all was good.

We'd picked up some road grime, a few bugs on the front

grill, but other than that, everything looked good. I was happy the rig was mine.

I checked the parking lot and decided a walk around the perimeter would get me ready for the next five hours of driving.

After ten minutes of walking, I headed back to the coach and noticed a few other cars had pulled into the lot. It was possible one of the vacant storefronts was being used for something. It didn't matter to me. I was ready to hit the road again.

I went back to the motorhome, unlocked the door, and opened it. That was a mistake. I should have been careful because Bob was waiting. As soon as he saw daylight, he darted out and ran.

I tried to grab him, but he was too fast. He was gone before I could reach him.

I had been warned. Molly had said don't let him escape. Jack had said the same thing. Don't let the cat get out. It'd be bad if he did.

He'd gotten out and it was bad.

I looked around and didn't see him anywhere. My guess was he wouldn't have run toward the highway—too much noise and too many cars.

He was probably under one of the ones parked nearby.

I started checking the cars in the lot and finally found him under an old Buick Electra. He was panting, obviously upset.

I got down on my hands and knees and tried to reach him. He didn't want to be touched. Each time I moved my hand in his direction, he bared his teeth and hissed, looking like he was ready to bite.

I didn't want to get bit but knew I had to get him. I belly

crawled toward him. When I did, he backed up further under the car, staying out of my reach.

I was lying on the ground, halfway under the Buick, when a voice behind me asked, "Hey mister, what are you doing under my grandma's car?"

I didn't answer.

"Listen mister, if my uncle finds you messing with Gramma's car, he'll shoot you."

That got my attention. I wriggled back out from under the car. A young black boy, probably about twelve years old, was standing behind me. He was wearing long black pants, a white shirt, a skinny black tie and looked like he was going to church.

He pointed again at the car.

"What are you doing under the car?"

"It's my cat. He ran up under there. I'm trying to get him back."

The kid shook his head. "You're not going to get him that way. Cats don't like it when you grab for them."

He was a smart kid.

"I'm finding that out. But I've got to get the cat back. He belongs to a friend."

The kid smiled. "I can do it for you if you pay me a dollar."

I doubted he could get the cat, but I'd sure let him try. "If you can get that cat back in my RV, I'll pay you ten."

He smiled. "It's a deal. Just do what I say. Where's your RV?"

I pointed to the motorhome.

"Nice. Go over and open the side door and leave it open. Then come over here and stand on the other side of my

135

gramma's car."

I did as he said, still not sure he was going to be able to get the cat. But I was going to let him try. He looked over at where I was standing by the big Buick and said, "Lie down so you're blocking the path between the front and rear wheels."

I did as he said.

When he saw that I was where he wanted me to be, he asked, "You ready?"

"Yeah, I'm ready."

"Good. Cover your ears!"

Before I could get my hands up to my ears, he reached into the car and pressed the horn on the old Buick. It sounded like a freight train coming down the road.

The horn trick worked. Bob immediately ran toward the motorhome, went up the steps and disappeared inside.

The kid walked over and closed the RV's door.

He came back to me and held out his hand. "Pay up."

I was amazed. And happy to pay.

I was pulling money from my wallet when a group of adults came out of the nearest storefront.

"What's going on here? Who are you and what are you doing with my grandson?"

It was an elderly black woman asking the questions.

I smiled and said, "Ma'am, this young man just saved my cat. I promised him a reward, and I'm paying him."

"Your cat? What's this all about?"

"It's alright, Grandma. This man's cat got out and I helped him get it back."

I nodded in agreement.

She looked at me. "What's your name?"

"Walker."

"Well, Mr. Walker, you need to be careful with that cat. They don't last long on the roads around here."

She looked at the motorhome. "You traveling in that?"

"Yes ma'am, I am. I'm headed to Mobile tonight and on to Florida tomorrow."

"You a criminal? Running from the law?"

"No ma'am. I'm not. I'm just trying to take that cat to a friend in Florida."

Looking again at my motorhome, she asked, "You got a bathroom and bed in there? And you're traveling alone, right?"

"Yes ma'am. Just me and the cat."

She looked behind her then back to me.

"Mr. Walker, my folks are gathered here today to see me off on a trip back to my home in Lucedale, Mississippi. We're waiting for the Trailways bus.

"It's a long way to go for an old gal like me, sitting in the cramped bus with all those strangers. People getting on and off at every little town. Some of them are not the kind you'd invite to dinner, if you know what I mean.

"It'll take the bus twelve hours to get to Lucedale. All that time, I'll be sitting in those hard plastic seats with all those strangers sitting around me.

"Wonder how long it'll take you to get there in that motorhome."

I wasn't sure why she was asking but didn't want to be rude so answered the best way I could.

"Ma'am, I'm not sure where Lucedale is. I don't know how

long it'd take me to get there. I'm trying to get to Mobile before dark. To do that, I need to get back on the road."

She smiled. "Sonny, how about this? Since my grandson did you a favor, maybe you'd do one for me. Let me ride with you to Lucedale. It's right on your way. I won't be any trouble.

"Riding in that RV of yours would be a lot easier on my poor, worn-out back than riding in a bus. It'd be Christian of you to let me ride along. I won't be any bother."

Her family was gathered around. One of them spoke up. "Momma, you don't know this guy. For all you know he might be an ax murderer. You can't just get in and ride off with him."

She turned to me. "Are you an ax murderer?"

"No ma'am, I'm not. But I need to get going pretty soon if I'm going to make Mobile by dark."

"Good, it's settled then. Grab my poke. Let's get on the road."

She pointed to the small suitcase on the ground beside her. I assumed it was her poke. After I picked it up, she smiled and said, "Mr. Walker, we haven't been properly introduced. I'm Mavis Tyler. My friends call my Mavis. You can call me that too."

She offered her hand. I shook it.

Still smiling, she said, "Jesus must have heard my prayers last night. I sure didn't want to ride in that bus for twelve hours. Thanks to you, I won't have to."

She turned and hugged the people standing behind her, saying a few words to each one.

As she was doing this, one of the men walked over and introduced himself. "Name's Earle Tyler. I'm a deputy sheriff here in Chicot County. That woman's my mother and we don't want to see nothing bad happen to her. You understand what I'm saying?"

I nodded. "Yeah, I do. I'll take good care of her. Give me your number and I'll call you when we get to Lucedale."

After we exchanged numbers, he repeated his warning. "Don't let nothing bad happen to her. You'll regret it if you do."

Mavis walked over. "Earle, leave Mr. Walker alone. I'm able to take care of myself. Don't you worry about me."

She went to the side door of my RV, and after I checked to make sure the cat was not waiting to jump out, I opened it and helped her in. She looked around, nodded her approval and settled down into the passenger seat.

After helping her with the seat belt I belted myself in and we pulled out of the parking lot with her family waving as we left.

Chapter 32

As soon as we got out on the road, Mavis said, "I love those children, but I'm happy to be heading back home. Just too busy with all those folks around.

"How about you, Walker, you have any young'ins?"

"No ma'am. Just me. And the cat."

"Well, one of these days you'll find the right woman and ya'll can have plenty of kids."

She stretched her legs. "This seat is a lot more comfortable than the ones on the bus. It smells better in here too."

Over the next hundred miles, she kept me entertained with stories about her family and the places we passed through. It turned out she had quite an interesting past and knew many colorful characters.

Time passed quickly.

As we approached the interstate coming out of Tallulah, she asked, "You said there was a bathroom in here?"

"Yes ma'am, there is. In the back. You want me to pull over so you can use it?"

"Yes, please. And after that, would you mind if I rested a bit on that bed back there?"

"No, not at all. Make yourself comfortable."

I pulled over into an empty parking lot. Mavis got up and went to the back. She took a few minutes to get arranged; then called out from the bedroom, "All done now. Ready to roll."

Out of Tallulah, we got onto I-20, which took us through Vicksburg toward Jackson, the road Jack had warned me about.

It wasn't bad at first, but as soon as we crossed the Mississippi River, traffic started building and I-20 deteriorated into a roller coaster ride. Long, slow ripples in the road caused cars and trucks to bounce up and down violently.

The locals were used to it; they drove ten miles over the limit. But not me. I had to slow down to fifty to keep the coach under control. Even at that speed, it sounded like the shelves in the back of the motorhome were about to come down.

It didn't seem to bother Mavis, but it got Bob's attention.

He came up front talking about it, wondering what was going on. He took the passenger seat beside me and kept talking. A series of meows that sounded like he wanted me to do something about the crazy road we were on.

I wished I could have, but it was out of my hands. It was up to the state of Mississippi to fix it. I had my doubts they would.

After about fifteen miles of heaving up and down, the road finally flattened out. Once I was sure the carnival ride was behind us, I brought the RV back up to speed and Bob settled down for a nap.

Halfway through Jackson, the GPS said my exit onto 49 south was approaching. I took it and was dumped out on a crowded four-lane road with backed-up traffic. There were stop lights at every intersection, and we caught them all.

I was frustrated, but it didn't seem to bother Bob. He continued to nap in the passenger seat, the sun streaming through the window warming his fur-covered body.

According to the route Jack had given me, I'd want to get fuel in Richland, Mississippi. Ten miles ahead.

Since leaving that morning, I'd driven three hundred miles and used little more than half a tank of gas. A quick calculation showed I was averaging about ten miles a gallon, about half what my Toyota pickup would have gotten.

I stopped at the U-Save gas station in Richland and filled up. It took 29 gallons and cost $91.17. I paid with my credit card.

Before going back into the coach, I checked the passenger window for Bob. He was asleep in the seat. I snuck around to the driver's door and hopped in. I didn't give him a chance to get out.

Mavis was still napping in the bed when I pulled back out onto the road. According to the GPS, we'd stay on 49 through Hattiesburg and then take 98 to Mobile.

We were on a four-lane road of rolling hills, bordered by farms and forests. The posted speed limit was sixty-five. Most everyone else was doing seventy or more. I stuck with my plan. Sixty-five and safe.

I wasn't going to make any friends going slow. Cars going way too fast would pull up behind me then whip around the first chance they got.

More than one driver signaled their displeasure. But I wasn't going to risk wrecking the Love Bus by going too fast on a country road just to keep someone who was in a hurry happy.

One car that came up behind us didn't pass. It followed for several miles staying just off our rear bumper. At first, I thought it was probably going to turn off onto a side road, but it didn't. It just stayed close behind. Too close for me.

I don't like tailgaters and was starting to get upset. I wasn't sure what I could do about it other than tap my brakes, hoping to get their attention. I tapped them. It made no difference. They stayed on our bumper for another ten miles.

Finally, the car, a late model dark blue Chevy sedan, pulled up beside us and the passenger rolled down his window.

I looked over and saw him pointing frantically toward the back of the Love Bus.

He was yelling, "Flat tire! Flat tire!"

Chapter 33

The steering didn't feel like I had a flat, but with six tires under the bus I didn't know what a flat would feel like. Wanting to be safe, I slowed and looked for a place to pull over. There was no shoulder, but there was a vacant gas station up ahead. When I got to it, I pulled in.

The car that had alerted me to the flat pulled in behind me and parked near the back of the RV.

I took a deep breath, hoping that none of the new tires had failed. I knew I didn't have a spare and doubted that anyone in the remote part of the state we were in would be able to fix a flat on a RV.

I took the keys from the ignition and went out to look. The driver and passenger of the car that had been following got out and walked toward me. I figured they were going to help.

But I was wrong. The shorter of the two men pulled a gun and said, "We're taking the motorhome. You're not coming with us."

I looked at the gun then at the two men. "Don't point that thing at me. It might go off."

The man with the gun said, "I don't want to shoot you. I just want the RV. Give me the keys and we won't hurt you."

I shook my head. "Are you crazy? I'm not going to let you take my RV. Put that gun away before you get hurt."

I was talking tough. Probably tougher than I should have been. But I didn't like having a gun pointed at me. There'd been many aimed in my direction in the past, and I never liked it. Back then, I was in uniform and carrying a rifle. I could shoot back when I needed to.

This time, I was unarmed. I wasn't going to let that stop me. I was going to figure a way out. When you can't shoot, you talk.

"What do you mean you're taking the motorhome?"

The man holding the gun said, "Just like I said. We're taking the motorhome. Give me the keys and you won't get hurt."

His partner, a tall skinny guy, made sure we stayed on the passenger side of the coach, out of sight of others on the road.

Still standing in front of me, the gunman said, "Slowly reach in your pocket and give me the keys."

I shook my head. "Don't have them. They're in the ignition."

I was lying. The keys were in my pocket, but I wasn't giving them up. Not yet, not before I figured out a way to disarm the man with the gun.

I'm no hero and didn't want to get shot. But Mavis and the cat were in the back of the RV. I couldn't risk either one of them getting hurt.

The man with the gun asked again, this time much more forcibly. "Give me the keys!"

I answered the same way I had before. "I don't have them. They're in the ignition. Go look for yourself."

He stared at me for a few seconds then told his partner to go check.

I was hoping to get a chance to go one-on-one with the gunman. It would be risky but less so than taking on both of them at the same time.

When the taller man opened the driver's door to look for the keys, I heard a humming sound then a loud crack. It sounded like a lighting strike.

The man crumpled to the ground shaking as if he were having a seizure.

The gunman looked over to see what was happening with his partner. When he did, I reached in, grabbed his gun hand and twisted it, keeping the barrel away from my body. I slammed the gun into the bridge of his nose, hearing bones break as I did.

Stunned by the blow, he loosened his grip and I took the gun from him. Using it as a club, I hit him full force on the side of his head just above his right ear. He dropped to the ground unconscious.

With him out of the way, I ran to the driver's door to see what had happened to the taller man.

Mavis was standing inside cackling with laughter while holding what looked like a police issue Taser.

She showed it to me. "This thing works a lot better than I thought it would. It dropped him like a bag of bricks."

I could hardly believe what I was seeing. "Where did you get that?"

She smiled. "I've had it with me all the time. You don't think my family would let me ride off with a stranger unless I was carrying something I could defend myself with."

The man on the ground was moaning. She looked down at him and said, "We need to do something with these two and get on our way. My people are waiting for me in Lucedale.

"Maybe we should teach them a lesson. Shoot them with their own gun. Leave them here to bleed out. The world would be better off."

I shook my head. "Mavis, you know we can't do that. We can't be killing them. That wouldn't be the right thing to do.

How about I put both of them in the trunk of their car and we call the police?"

She crossed her arms. "You're letting them off easy. But if that's what you want, go ahead and do it. I still say we should shoot them."

I was pretty sure her talk about shooting was for the benefit of the man she had tazed. She wanted him to know things could have gone a lot worse.

I fished the keys out of the taller man's pockets, went over to their car and opened the trunk. I went back to the man, grabbed him, and dragged him to his car. Making sure no one was watching, I shoved him in the trunk.

The shorter man was still on the ground, groaning, blood flowing freely from his nose.

Mavis suggested I give him a taste of the Taser. She said it'd make it easier to get him in the car.

I wasn't so sure. He didn't look like he was going to put up a fight. He was hurting.

I kicked his shoe to get his attention. "You going to fight?"

He groaned. "No, I've had enough. Don't taze me. I'll get in."

Mavis tazed him anyway.

After he quit twitching, I put him in the trunk and slammed it shut.

There was a cell phone in their car. I used it to call 911 and report a carjacking on Highway 49, near Collins, Mississippi.

I gave the operator the description of the vehicle along with the plate number. I told her the two assailants could be found in the trunk. The keys to the car along with the gun they used were under the driver's floor mat.

When she asked my name, I ended the call and left the

phone in the car.

It was time to get back on the road.

Chapter 34

"Mavis, how'd you get a police Taser? Where'd you learn to use it?"

She smiled. "Remember my son, Earle? The man you met back in Lake Village? After I got into a little trouble with a pop gun I was carrying, he took it away and gave me the Taser. Said not to use it except in an emergency.

"So when I saw that guy pull a gun on you, I got it out and was hoping to get a shot. When his partner opened the door, I couldn't miss.

"Did you see how he twitched and wet his pants when I hit him with it? Funniest thing I've seen in a long time."

She was grinning when she said, "This is turning out to be the best trip ever."

I was glad she was enjoying herself and relieved that the three of us had gotten away unhurt. It could have ended quite differently if she hadn't been with me.

"Mavis, I don't think those guys were kidding around. Do you think we should call Earle and let him know what happened? Him being a deputy and all?"

She shook her head. "Heavens no! We don't want him knowing about this. He worries enough as it is. If he finds out I tazed two people and locked them in the trunk of a car, he might put us both in jail. We need to keep this to ourselves."

I nodded. "I'm good with that. The last thing I want to do is get mixed up with the law in Mississippi."

We traveled in silence for the next thirty miles, both of us probably thinking about the men and the gun. I was wondering if we should go back and let them out of the

151

trunk. If it had been hot, I would have. But it was a cool day and the police had been alerted. They'd probably be okay.

My train of thought was interrupted when Mavis said, "Lucedale is just ahead. Take a right at the next flashing light."

I followed her directions through the tiny town until we reached a dirt driveway leading to an older wood-sided home with a large covered porch. Three young boys were sitting on the porch swing watching as we pulled up in the big RV.

The kids stood and looked at their parents, not sure about the big bus pulling into their yard. When they saw Mavis wave from the passenger window, they understood. "Grandma's here! Grandma's here."

She nodded in their direction. "I love those boys, but they're a real handful. Still, it pleasures my heart to see them so happy."

She turned to me. "Walker, you're invited to come in and eat with us. We've got plenty of food and plenty of room. You could park here and stay the night if you want."

It was kind of her to ask, but I declined.

"Mavis, I appreciate the offer, but I'm trying to get to Mobile tonight. So as much as I'd like to stay, I've got to keep going."

I looked at the three boys who had come out to greet their grandma and I thought of something. The tent. The big blue one that I had stored in one of the bays back when I left Toad Suck. I wondered if the boys would want it.

"Mavis, you think your grandsons would like a tent? It's almost new, and if you think they'd want it, I'd be happy to give it to them."

"A tent? Is it big enough for all three of those boys?"

"Yes, ma'am, it is. It's plenty big and easy to set up."

She thought for a moment then said, "Get it out, see if they want it. And remember our little secret. Don't tell my kinfolk anything about what happened on the road."

We stepped out of the RV and while she was hugging her three grandsons, I pulled the tent out of the storage bay. It didn't look like much the way it was folded up. I decided maybe it would be better if I set it up for the boys.

Mavis had the same idea. She came over with her three grandsons and said, "Boys, this is Mister Walker. He's brought you a tent."

The taller of the three, a young man who looked to be about thirteen, asked, "A tent? Can we set it up?"

I nodded. "Sure, just show me where."

He pointed to a bare patch of lawn under an old oak tree. "That'd be a good spot."

I looked at Mavis to make sure it was okay. She nodded her approval.

The boys and I carried the tent over, and after spreading it out on the ground under the tree, I showed them how to set it up. It took less than three minutes and they did most of the work.

As soon as it was up, the three went inside and I could hear them talking about how it was going to be their new club house and how they were going to sleep in it that night and every night after.

They were so excited I figured I'd seen the last of them. But I was wrong. The boys came out, ran over to me, and each one shook my hand and thanked me. They went over to their grandmother and thanked her as well with the youngest one saying, "This is the best day ever, Grandma."

153

They were all smiles. It was good to see.

I locked up the cargo bay and headed to the RV's side door. Mavis was there waiting for me.

"Mister Walker, thank you for the ride and the tent. The boys sure like it. Now that you know where we live, feel free to drop by any time. Maybe we'll go out and find some more bad guys."

I laughed and told her I looked forward to seeing her again. After we hugged, I got back in the Love Bus.

Before I drove off, I remembered to check on Bob. He was in the back bedroom sleeping with his head on my pillow, one of his paws over his face to block out the light. If he hadn't looked so contented, I would have made him find another place to sleep. I didn't want him drooling on my pillow.

He'd had a hard day, so I let him be.

Chapter 35

The GPS said I was just forty-eight miles from the Bass Pro store on the other side of Mobile. I was planning to meet up with Jack and Jean and spend the night there. It should have been an easy drive.

But it wasn't. Traffic got heavier and heavier as I got closer to Mobile. The two-lane road I was on, which was the only way in from the north, had a stoplight about every other mile. Almost as soon as I got clear of one, I'd have stop at another.

It was slow going and there were a lot of impatient drivers on the road who didn't want to be stuck behind a motorhome. I didn't blame them; if I were in a car, I wouldn't want to be stuck behind me either.

After spending way too much time to cover just thirty miles, I finally reached the Mobile city limits. Getting off the two-lane road, I got up on I-65 and west for eight miles, then took the exit to I-10 east going toward the Mobile Bay Tunnel.

Traffic on I-10 was moving a lot faster than it had been on the country roads and there were a lot more cars. It was just after five in the evening, and rush hour was in full force. To play it safe, I kept to the far right lane, listening for the GPS to tell me when to get off.

I'd already driven ten hours with just three stops—one of which involved gun play. The sun was setting and I needed a bathroom break. But first I had to get through the Mobile Bay Tunnel.

Going through it in an oversized vehicle like a motorhome would be a challenge. The RV was tall and wide, and the tunnel wasn't. But I didn't have a choice. The tunnel was the only way to get from Mobile into Florida.

As I got closer, road signs warned of the tunnel ahead and flashing lights said to slow down. I slowed, but most of the cars around me didn't. Some of them sped up. When I finally got to the tunnel entrance, the lanes narrowed and I was funneled down a steep slope into the dark shaft.

Being in the far right lane, I was close to the white tiles of the tunnel walls and just inches under the curving roof. I knew that if for any reason I needed to veer to the right, I'd be in trouble. The waters of the Gulf of Mexico were above me, the hard walls of the tunnel were on my right and fast moving traffic to my left.

I hunched over the wheel, worried that the RV's roof might scrape the tunnel's low ceiling. But I shouldn't have been. There were taller and wider eighteen wheelers ahead of me and they had no problem getting through. Still, I kept both hands on the wheel, my eyes on the road ahead and ignored the cars and big trucks passing on my left, just inches from my door.

Finally, after what seemed far longer than it actually was, I could see the light at the other end. Other drivers could see it as well, and those familiar with the area sped up, racing to where the road rose steeply up from the ocean floor onto the Mobile Bay causeway.

Coming up out of the tunnel, I was surprised by what I saw. The road ahead was bounded on both sides by the sea, with waves crashing just beyond the pavement. The smell of salty air was strong and in the distance I could see shipyards with massive boats under construction. There was an aircraft carrier and a submarine docked at a pier up ahead on my right. It looked like they were tourist attractions open to the public.

If I'd had time, I would have stopped to take a closer look.

But I was too busy to take in the sights. I was driving a six-ton rig across a narrow strip of pavement surrounded on both sides by water. A wrong move by me or any of the thousands of others crossing the causeway ahead of me would have been disastrous.

I was careful. I didn't want to be in a wreck. Sixty was the posted speed limit and that's all I was going to do. Maybe even a little less.

According to Jack, the exit that would take me to the Bass Pro parking lot was just a few miles beyond the tunnel. With all the traffic around me, I was worried I'd miss it. I shouldn't have been. It was clearly marked, and the Bass Pro building sat like a massive hundred-forty-thousand-square-foot log castle rising up on a hill above the interstate.

I took the exit, followed the signs, and quickly reached the Bass Pro parking lot.

Chapter 36

In the Bass Pro lot, I followed the signs leading to the RV parking area. There weren't a lot of RVs there and it didn't take me long to find Jack and Jean's rig. I parked next to it, leaving an empty space between the two RVs.

After killing the motor, I went back to let Bob know we were in for the evening. He wasn't on the bed and I hadn't seen him on my way to the bedroom. I wasn't too worried. Cats are pretty good at hiding and knowing that I hadn't opened the outside doors since last checking on him, I was pretty sure he hadn't gotten out.

He showed up when I walked into the bathroom. He had been digging in his litter, and when he saw me, he hopped out and trotted over. After sniffing my shoe, he surprised me when he rubbed his head against my leg. We'd been together for less than twenty-four hours and I didn't expect him to have anything to do with me. But if he wanted to be friends, I'd sure play along.

I bent over and stroked his back. He flicked his stub of a tail then trotted off in the general direction of the bedroom.

After I took care of my bathroom business, I checked on his food and water. I didn't want him to go hungry. It might affect his newly found fondness for me.

The night before, Jack had said that Bass Pro had a restaurant and that he and Jean were planning to eat there. Since I was hungry, I decided to check it out. Before heading over, I let Bob know I was leaving and asked him not to try to escape when I came back. He didn't reply.

Stepping out of the Love Bus, I noticed the inside lights in Jack and Jean's coach weren't on. Either they had already gone to bed or were in Bass Pro. Not wanting to disturb them if they were sleeping, I headed across the parking lot toward the main entrance of the store.

When I walked in, I was amazed. Over a hundred and forty thousand square feet of retail shopping space filled with everything you can imagine for outdoor fun. Hiking, camping, boating, hunting, fishing; you name it, they had it.

I could have spent a few days there and not seen it all. But at the time, I wasn't interested in shopping. I wanted food.

I headed to the restaurant and was happy to see there wasn't a line. As I looked around for a table, my phone chimed with an incoming call from Jack. He had seen me walk in and invited me to join him and Jean for dinner.

"We're in a booth by the back window. I'll stand up and wave."

It wasn't hard to find him. He was the only man standing near the back of the restaurant waving at me. When he saw me nod in his direction, he sat and waited for me to join them.

There were four seats at the table. Jack and Jean were sitting across from each other. I took the seat next to Jean because men don't sit next to each other if they can avoid it. We ordered our meals and while we waited for our food, discussed our travels.

Jack said they had arrived about an hour earlier and had an uneventful trip. They had stopped in Mississippi to gas up and found a little cafe where they had fresh-caught catfish and hush puppies for lunch. They said I should give it a try if I was ever in the area.

When they asked about my drive, I told them things went well. I hadn't got lost. The motorhome hadn't broken down, and the traffic wasn't all that bad. The roller coaster roads around Jackson were as described.

I didn't mention Bob's escape or Mavis or the attempted carjacking.

Our meals arrived with our plates piled high with food. We dug in, making small talk as we ate.

After we finished and our dishes were cleared away, Jack said, "Tomorrow will be easier. We'll stay on I-10 for three hundred miles until we get to the Florida Georgia Parkway. There, we'll turn south and follow the road to Chiefland. That'll take us to Manatee Springs, where we'll camp for the night.

"It's about four hundred miles total. Ten hours of driving. Plenty for one day. We'll spend the night at the Springs and the next morning it'll be two hundred miles to Venice."

When he paused, Jean took over. "I think you'd like the Springs. The campground is just ten miles off the main highway and it's right on the Suwanee River.

"The springs pump out a hundred million gallons of clear, cool water daily. There's a boardwalk that goes through the lowlands and follows the springs all the way out to the river. Along the way, you'll see Manatees playing in the water.

"The campsites are pretty nice too. Shaded and spaced far apart. Plenty of privacy. If you get hungry, they have a small cafe where you can get a hot meal. It's one of our favorite places to camp."

It sounded like a good place to stop for the night. "Will I need a reservation?"

"Probably not. But better to have one than to get turned away at the gate. If you can get on the internet, use ReserveAmerica to find a spot."

I nodded. "When I get back to the motorhome, I'll do that."

Jack jumped in and said, "Be sure to gas up in the morning before you get back on the road. Fuel prices in Florida will be about fifteen cents a gallon more than they are here."

He looked at Jean. "If we leave at seven, we should make Manatee Springs by five without having to push it. It's an easy drive, most of it on long stretches of boring interstate."

I smiled. "I'll take boring. Better than the excitement I had today."

Jean looked at me, no longer smiling. "Something happened? Tell us about it."

I should have kept my mouth shut, but I didn't. "It started in Lake Village. I stopped at a shopping center to stretch my legs. I got out, took and walk, went back to the RV. When I opened the door, the cat jumped out.

"I tried to catch him, but couldn't. He was gone in a flash. I thought I'd lost him, but a young boy came over and said he'd help me get him back if I'd pay him a dollar. I didn't think he'd have any chance of getting the cat back, but I let him try.

"Turned out, he knew what he was doing. It didn't take him long to get the cat back in the RV unharmed. I gave him ten dollars as a reward.

"His grandmother had been inside one of the stores and when she saw me giving him money she came out and asked what was going on.

"I told her about the cat and how her grandson had helped me get him back. She said he was always doing things like that, helping people.

"She saw my motorhome and asked where I was going. When I told her Mobile, she said she was taking a bus to Lucedale. She said it was on my way, and after she explained it would be a lot easier for her to ride with me in the RV than to

162

spend twelve hours on a hard plastic seat on the bus, I gave in. I agreed to give her a ride.

"We left and she kept me entertained with her stories about the people and places we passed through, although I don't know how much of what she said was true."

Jean stopped me. "Do you make a habit of picking up strange women? That can't be safe."

I shook my head. "It wasn't like that. She wasn't hitchhiking or anything. I was in the parking lot looking for the cat. If it hadn't been for her grandson, the cat would have been long gone. After he helped me, there was no way I could turn her down."

She nodded. "That was nice of you. But you should be careful about picking up strangers."

"I know. Don't pick up hitchhikers. But this was different. Her family was there, including her son, a deputy sheriff. He was more worried about me than her. I think he knew she could take care of herself."

I could have told them about how she had used a Taser to put down the attempted carjacking. But I didn't. The fewer people who knew of our involvement, the better.

Jack nodded in my direction. "Walker, I've been meaning to ask you something. Jean says I shouldn't. She says it's none of my business. But I have to ask anyway.

"Most of the RVers we meet are like us. Retired, and older.

"But you're a young guy. Traveling alone.

"What do you do that gives you that kind of freedom? If it's none of my business, just say so. I won't take offense."

I smiled. "Jack, I don't mind sharing my story.

"Up until three weeks ago, I was married and had a good job with a Fortune 500 company. Then my wife surprised me by filing for divorce. She said she was doing me a favor. Giving me my freedom. We didn't have any kids, so it was quick and easy. All I had to do was sign the papers and walk away.

"We split everything down the middle, except for the house, which her daddy owned. She stayed in it, and I had to find another place to stay.

"About the same time, the company I was working for announced it was closing. Everyone was laid off, including me.

"I was still looking for a place to stay when a friend at the plant told me the company had a motorhome they needed to sell. It was offered to me at a great price, and since I needed a roof over my head, I bought it.

"I've gone from having a good job, being married, and living in a nice house to being divorced, unemployed, and living in an RV. It definitely wasn't part of my plans."

Jean reached out and put her hand on mine. "So how are you holding up?"

I thought about it before I answered. "Pretty good, I guess. The motorhome came along at the right time. I never thought I'd own one, but now that I do, I like having it. It gives me a sense of freedom. No matter where I stop I have a place to stay."

Jack nodded. "We get that same feeling every time we hit the road. Can't imagine life without an RV. The only downside is the cost of fuel. But the way we figure it, we make up for it by not having to pay for hotel rooms.

"We get to sleep in our own bed every night and don't have to worry about bed bugs or who slept there the night before."

He folded his napkin. "I'm itching to go look at the

camping supplies they have here. Maybe they'll have a few things I want."

Jean laughed. "I'm sure they will. But not many things you need. I'm going with you to make sure you don't go crazy."

The waitress put our dinner bills on the table and I quickly snatched them up.

"Walker, no need to do that. We invited you."

"Jack, you and Jean have helped me so much on this trip. Getting the meal is the least I can do."

Jean smiled. "It isn't necessary, but thanks. We appreciate it."

She stood and said, "If you'll excuse me, I need to follow Jack through the store. Want to join us?"

I shook my head. "Thanks, but no. I think I'll just wander around a bit before I head back to the RV. I've got that cat in there and need to check on him."

I spent thirty minutes exploring Bass Pro and found plenty of things I'd love to have but nothing I really needed.

When I got back to the motorhome, I was thinking about Bob's earlier escape attempt. Instead of just walking up and opening the same door he had gotten out of before, I came up with what I hoped would be a better plan.

I walked to the side door, the one he had escaped from, and tapped it to get his attention. Then, assuming he had heard me and was waiting at the door, I snuck around to the driver's door and quickly climbed in.

I was in and had the door closed before he realized what was happening. My plan worked. Not sure it would work the next time, but it had then.

Bob looked up from the side door where he had been waiting for me and yawned. He acted like I hadn't fooled him, but I knew I had. "Bob, I beat you this time. You didn't get out."

He stretched and said, "Murrpff," conceding that I won the round. But maybe he'd get me on the next one.

He came over, bumped his head against my leg, and rubbed my ankle. He wanted me to know we were still friends.

Remembering what Jack had said about getting a reservation at Manatee Springs, I powered up my laptop and went to the Reserve America website.

There were five campsites available for the following day. I reserved the one closest to the springs. Twenty dollars for the night. Not bad.

With the campsite taken care of and my belly full of food, it was time to get ready for bed.

I locked the doors, pulled the blinds, and moved to the back bedroom. Bob followed and took his position on my pillow.

I was about to move him when my phone chimed with an incoming call from Molly. She probably wanted to know how Bob and I were getting along.

I answered on the third ring.

Chapter 37

"Walker, you still driving?"

"No, I parked about an hour ago. Made it to the other side of Mobile."

"That far, huh? You're making good time. How's it going with Bob? Is he driving you crazy?"

"No, not yet. He slept most of the day, ate a little food, used his litter box, and seems pretty content."

"Good to hear. I was worried about him. But there's another reason I wanted to talk to you.

"I got a call today from Detective Tim Kerber of the Boston Police Department. He wanted to know why Tucker had called me.

"When I asked why the police were interested, he said Tucker had been murdered. Shot three times.

"They found his cell phone and were checking his recent calls. My number showed up."

I was stunned. Not only by the death of someone I knew from the plant, but by it being so soon after him trying to find the whereabouts of the Love Bus, my new home.

"What'd you tell him?"

"The truth. That Tucker had called asking about the motorhome. He wanted to know who had it and where it was parked.

"The detective didn't know if the calls mattered but said he would get back to me if they needed more information.

"I didn't tell them your name or that Tucker had said he may have left something in the RV. But it's worrisome. Him calling me then getting murdered the same day."

"Yep, it is. If the police call back and want to contact me, give them my email address but not my phone number. I don't want to get any calls while I'm driving, especially from the police."

As I was telling her this, Bob started howling.

Molly could hear him on her end and knew what he wanted. "Sounds like he's telling you it's time for his catnip. It's part of his routine. A little catnip snack before he starts his nightly prowl."

He continued to cry and it was starting to get on my nerves.

"What do I need to do to get him to pipe down?"

She laughed. "Check his bag. The one with his toys. You'll find a small plastic baggy with what looks like grass in it. Take out about a tablespoon and crush it up between your fingers.

"Then put it on a plate and show it to him. He'll scarf it up and it'll mellow him out for a few hours. But be warned, once he trains you to do it, he'll want it every night."

I laughed. "As long as it gets him to shut up, I'll do it. It'll be your sister's problem after Monday."

"That's when you think you'll get there? Monday?"

"Yeah, unless something goes wrong with the Love Bus. So far, no problems, other than it uses a lot of gas. I'll call your sister when I have a better idea of when I'm going to get to her place."

"Good. She'll be happy to see Bob. I'll call her tomorrow and let her know.

"Walker, I've got to go. Need to deal with the kids. If I hear anything else about Tucker's death, I'll let you know. Bye."

She ended the call.

Harvey Tucker had been killed. He'd spent his last day alive trying to find the Love Bus. The same day that someone tried to steal it.

Something was definitely going on.

Chapter 38

It was Sunday morning and hard to believe that four days earlier I had been living in a tent.

Since then, I had moved into a house on wheels, left Arkansas, and was currently camping out in the parking lot of a Bass Pro superstore near Mobile, Alabama.

I was on my way to Englewood, Florida to deliver a cat named Mango Bob to a woman I'd never met.

The sun was already up and I needed to get on the road if I wanted to reach Manatee Springs before dark. But I couldn't get up. For some reason, I felt pinned to the bed. A heavy weight was pressing down on my chest.

I would have been worried that I was having a heart attack if the weight hadn't been purring.

It was the cat. He was sleeping on top of me.

I slowly moved my legs trying my best not to disturb him. He rewarded me by extending a claw into my belly. Not deep enough to hurt, just a warning.

It was like he was saying, "Don't mess with me while I sleep."

I didn't want to, but I needed to get out of bed. "Bob, it's time for me to get up."

He didn't seem to care. He didn't move.

"I'm going to have to move you, don't use your claws."

He yawned and said, "Murrrf."

I didn't know if that meant he would or wouldn't dig in, but I was about to find out.

I slowly lifted him off my chest and set him down on the

171

bed beside me. I quickly rolled out of bed and stood. Looking down at him, I saw him open one eye and heard him say, "Murrph."

Then he moved onto the spot where I had been sleeping. I guess I had warmed it up to his satisfaction.

I went to the kitchen and peeked out the window. Jack and Jean's RV was gone. They had already pulled out. Twenty minutes later, after a quick breakfast, I was ready to follow in their tracks.

Remembering Jack's advice, I stopped for gas at Sam's Club. I pumped twenty-five gallons of regular, setting me back almost a hundred dollars.

Leaving Sam's, I took the ramp back onto I-10 East toward Tallahassee. The GPS showed two hundred seventy miles until my next turn.

I set the cruise control to sixty-five and stayed in the right lane.

The skies were blue, the sun was shining and there was no wind pushing the motorhome around. Good times.

After an hour of driving, I decided that I-10 in Florida should be the model for all interstate highways. It was perfectly flat with wide shoulders, a grassy median, and in tiptop shape.

But driving on it was boring as hell.

All I had to do was set the cruise control and point the steering wheel and try not to doze off.

After four hours, the boredom finally got to me. I pulled into a rest area near Monticello. I needed to get out and stretch my legs, but first I wanted to check on Bob. There was really no reason to, but I didn't want to leave the motorhome without knowing where he was.

I went to the back and found him still on the bed, sleeping. I hoped it meant I wouldn't have to worry about him trying to escape when I went out. Or when I came back in.

Going outside, I locked the door behind me. The few things I owned were in the motorhome and I didn't want to risk losing them. Looking around, I saw that there was a two-mile nature trail around the rest area. As far as I could tell, there weren't any other people on it, so I decided to check it out.

It turned out to be way better than I expected. A well-groomed trail that looped around a small pond, most of the way shaded by tall palms. It was only after I got to the end of it that I noticed the sign that said, "Beware of Alligators."

I hadn't seen any, but it didn't mean they weren't there.

On my way back to the coach, I stopped in the vending area and got a Coke from the machine along with an assortment of Florida tourist brochures. The Coke's caffeine would keep me awake. The brochures would give me something to read at night.

Back at the Love Bus, I tapped on the side door to get Bob's attention then snuck over to the driver's door and opened it.

He was there waiting for me; he had figured out my plan. But he didn't try to escape. He just looked at me and said, "Murrrph."

I think he was telling me he could have gotten out if he wanted to. I had no doubt. He could have.

It was lunchtime; I put together a peanut butter and jelly sandwich, added a few chips, and ate. It wasn't health food, but it was better than driving on an empty stomach.

After lunch, I checked the freezer to make sure the TV

dinners I'd bought back at Walmart were still frozen. They were. One of them would be my dinner that night.

Refreshed from the walk and the snack, I pulled the motorhome back out onto I-10 and set the cruise control to sixty-five. It'd be another two hours before I got to my exit then another two hours on country roads before I reached the state park.

There wasn't much to say about that part of the drive. Good roads, not much traffic. Boredom with a capital B.

Chapter 39

After driving three hundred boring miles on I-10, it was a relief to finally get to Highway 19 South, also known as the Florida/Georgia Parkway. It was the road that would take me to my night's destination.

To celebrate, I stopped at the Chevron station at the off-ramp and fueled up. Another hundred dollars spent on gas.

After paying at the pump, I went inside and bought two bags of peanut M&Ms. Something to snack on while on the road.

Bob was still asleep when I got back in the coach. He didn't bother to try to escape. He was adapting well.

I grabbed a bottle of cold water from the fridge. With it and my M&Ms, I was ready to hit the road again.

Pulling out of the Chevron station, I headed south. The GPS said it'd be another two hours before the day's drive was over.

According to one of the brochures I'd picked up at the rest area, the Florida Georgia parkway was once the main road travelers used to get to South Florida. But with the advent of the interstate system, most people no longer bothered with the parkway. They preferred the high speeds on the interstate.

That meant very little traffic. I liked it that way.

The Parkway's road surface was in surprisingly good condition and looked to have been recently repaved with wide shoulders added to both sides. The terrain was mostly flat, surrounded by pine forests and the occasional cow pasture.

Every few miles, I'd see remnants of old Florida;

abandoned mom and pop motels well past their glory days.

With so little traffic it wasn't surprising there weren't many tourist attractions left in the area. No theme parks, no sideshows and no beach bunnies. Just tropical wilderness with small towns every fifteen to twenty miles.

After two hours of driving, I reached Chiefland, a town of about six thousand hardy souls. Its main attraction was Manatee Springs State Park, my final stop of the day. I followed the signs and eventually reached the park's gate.

A ranger greeted me. Our conversation went something like this. "Welcome to Manatee Springs. You staying with us tonight?"

"Yeah, I have a reservation. The name's Walker."

The ranger looked me up on his computer. "Says here you are staying just the one night. Is that correct?"

"Yes sir, just one night."

"Okay, you're going to be in loop A, site ninety-three. Drive slowly into the park and take the first right. Your site is about halfway around the loop.

"We lock the park gates at sunset and unlock them at dawn. Once they're locked, no one can enter or leave the campground.

"If an emergency comes up, you'll have to call the camp host to get the gate opened.

"Any questions?"

I had just one.

"Do I need to worry about alligators?"

He laughed. "There's always the chance of a gator just about anywhere in Florida, but we haven't had a problem with them here. At least not lately.

"Your biggest issue will be with the squirrels and raccoons.

They'll get into your food if you leave any out overnight. They'll try to get into your RV if you leave your doors open."

I told the ranger I'd be sure to keep my doors closed and my food locked away. I thanked him for his help and headed to my campsite.

It was easy to find. First road to the right and then about halfway around the loop. The site was under large shade trees with no nearby neighbors. Just the way I liked it.

I drove past, stopped, and backed in like Jack had shown me. Satisfied with my parking job, I killed the motor and went back to see Bob.

He was pretty much where I expected him to be. On the bed. I updated him on our status. "Bob, we've stopped for the day. You can get up and move around if you want."

I got his standard all-around reply, "Murrpff," followed by an odd sound as he stretched and yawned at the same time.

He jumped down from the bed and went to the bathroom to check his food and water. Seeing that both bowls were full, he bumped my leg, stretched again, and headed to the kitchen. I followed.

Without asking, he jumped up on the back of the couch and looked out the window. Just as the ranger had said, there were plenty of squirrels outside moving around on the ground and in the trees.

Their activity immediately got Bob's attention. He moved up against the closed window and started making a clicking sound in his throat. I'd had a cat before and knew it meant he was making a plan to give chase.

But I wasn't going to let him out. Certainly not to go after squirrels in a state park. The ranger might frown on it.

Still, with the weather outside being so nice, I opened all the windows to air things out. There were screens to keep the bugs out and, hopefully, Bob in.

With the windows open, sounds of birds and squirrels filled the coach along with the scent of tropical plants. Bob came alive when he saw a furry tail moving on a nearby branch. He stared at it for a few moments then started making the clicking sound again. His stubby tailed twitched as he worked out a plan of attack. I watched, hoping the window screens would hold him if he decided to make a move.

It'd been a few hours since our last stop and I needed to freshen up. After a quick trip to the bathroom, I decided to go outside and check out the park.

With Bob focused on the squirrel at the window, it was easy to sneak out without him trying to escape.

Outside, I walked around the coach to make sure there weren't any problems. A quick check showed all was good. Nothing was leaking, the tires still had air, and no parts were falling off.

I was actually surprised I had made it so far without any issues.

Since I was only spending one night, I didn't bother to hook up to campground water. My freshwater tank was half full. More than enough for the rest of my journey.

I did need to hook up to shore power since I wanted to use the microwave to cook dinner. I unlocked the utility compartment and connected the power cable to the thirty-amp outlet on the campground electric pole.

When I flipped the breaker, I heard the microwave beep inside the coach, telling me the power was on.

Success.

Before heading out for a walk, I locked all the doors, something I wanted to get in the habit of doing. I wasn't expecting a break-in at the campground, but it was possible. There'd been one just two nights earlier at Toad Suck.

The map the ranger had given me showed a trail about forty yards beyond my campsite that would take me down to the springs. I decided to give it a go.

I followed it for about a hundred yards through a tropical forest until it ended at a large open plaza. On the far side several people were leaning against a metal railing looking down, presumably at the springs the campground was famous for.

Jack and Jean were with them.

I walked up and said, "You guys been here long?"

Jack turned at my voice and smiled. "Hey, Walker. Glad to see you made it. We got here about an hour ago. How was your drive?"

"Not bad. The coach drove well and other than the boredom on I-10, it was easy going."

Jean smiled. "You didn't pick up any hitchhikers, did you?"

"No, not today. But if there'd been a pretty girl in distress, I probably would have stopped."

She laughed. "Men, always thinking about the same thing."

She pointed to the spring. "So what do you think about this place?"

"I like it so far. Camping in a tropical forest with great weather."

She smiled. "If you like this, you're going to love Florida in the winter. The further you travel south the nicer it gets."

She pointed to the springs. "There's a manatee down there."

Looking at where she was pointing, I could see the head of a very large creature moving slowly in the water. Beside it were two smaller ones.

Someone in the crowd shouted, "Babies! That one has babies!"

We watched as the manatees slowly moved around, swimming with their snouts above the water and their massive bodies following.

Jean smiled. "They come up here from the Suwanee River. Sometimes you'll see as many as ten at a time. They like the warmer water this time of year."

A family with small children walked up to the viewing area. I moved back so they could get a closer look.

Jean moved back with me. "Have you been on the boardwalk yet? It goes all the way out to the river."

"No, I haven't. But a long walk sounds good. How do I get to it?"

"Just follow me. I'll walk with you."

Chapter 40

"What about Jack? Isn't he coming with us?"

"Don't worry about him; he'll be along in a minute.

"Right now it's just me and you. Unless you're embarrassed to be walking with an old woman like me?"

"Jean, you're not much older than me."

"Thanks for the compliment. But I've got grandchildren almost as old as you. Not that it means I'm old. I can probably out walk you any day."

She paused then said, "I've been thinking about what you said about your divorce and losing your job.

"That's a lot to take on. If you ever want to talk about it, give me a call." She handed me a card with her phone number.

"Jean, I appreciate the offer. I just might take you up on it. But what will Jack think if I call you?"

"Don't worry about him. He likes you. In fact, he's probably going to want to keep in touch with you. He needs a fishing and RV buddy.

"He's been retired from the force for almost five years and most of his close buddies have gotten old or moved on. He has room for a new friend in his life, especially one who shares his interest in motorhomes.

"You should see how happy he is when he talks about showing you things or when he gets to help route your trip.

"It gives him something to do. Makes him feel good that someone still values his expertise."

I was glad to hear it. Jack had helped me a lot on that trip. I'd hoped I wasn't a burden.

As we continued along the boardwalk through the cypress swamp, I asked, "You mentioned Jack had retired from the force? What do you mean?"

She looked over her shoulder, checking to make sure our conversation wasn't bothering anyone. We were walking on the boardwalk, a quiet sanctuary built over wetlands. She didn't want to disturb others. No one was in sight, so she continued. "Jack was a police officer for thirty years in Boston. He started out as a rookie cop and ended up as a detective supervisor."

"Really? Jack was a Boston police detective?"

"Yep, and not just a detective. He was a detective supervisor, which meant all the detectives in his district reported directly to him.

"He handled lots of major cases, some you've probably heard of. But it was hard on him, seeing the underbelly of society. When he retired, he wanted to get as far away from Boston as he could. That's how we ended up in Colorado.

"Lately the cold winters there have been bothering him. He's been hinting about moving to Florida permanently."

I could understand why someone living in Colorado would be thinking about moving south. But that's not what I wanted to talk about. I was more interested in what Jean had said about Jack being a former Boston detective. With his contacts there, he might be able to find out more about Tucker's death.

"Jean, do you think Jack would mind if I asked him some questions about a police investigation? It involves the murder of someone who used to travel in my motorhome."

"Honey, that's the kind of thing he lives for. I'm sure he'd want to know all about it. All you have to do is ask."

Chapter 41

We were at the end of the boardwalk overlooking the Suwanee River when Jack caught up with us.

Jean pointed to the setting sun over the peaceful waters. "Quite a sight."

I agreed. "You were right. This is an amazing place. Like stepping back in time."

Jack put his arm around his wife. "This is one of our favorite spots. We stop here every time we travel this way.

"I keep promising her that one day we'll stay longer. Maybe take the kayak tours the park offers. But I'm always in a hurry to get to Venice."

Jean looked at him. "Yeah, you're like a man on a mission when we get on the road. You map out the route, set the schedule then worry about getting off track.

"You forget that we are retired. We don't have any schedules or deadlines we have to meet."

Jack sighed. "You're right. I treat these road trips like a military campaign. I'll try to do better next time."

She smiled and gave him a hug. "That's all I ask."

She looked at me. "Walker, wasn't there something you wanted to ask Jack?"

That was my cue. "Jack, Jean was telling me you were with the Boston police. That sounds pretty interesting."

He nodded. "It was. Until politics got in the way of police work. We ended up spending more time keeping the mayor happy than getting criminals off the street.

"After thirty years, I wasn't in sync with the college boys

running the department. It was time for me to leave. I was lucky. I got out with my pension, my health, and my sanity. Jean stuck with me through it all. I'm very thankful for that."

Jean grabbed his hand. "Let's head back. It's getting dark. I'm getting hungry."

We followed the boardwalk back through the cypress trees then followed the gravel trail past the springs. From there we headed back in the direction of our campsites.

"I'm in loop A. Where are you guys?"

"We're in loop A too. Close to the restrooms. You want to come over and plan out tomorrow's route?"

"Jack, I don't want to impose, but I'd like to talk to you about a Boston police investigation. It might involve my motorhome. Might even be related to the attempted break-in of yours."

He stopped and looked at me. "You're kidding, right?"

"No, I'm serious. It might not be anything, but a Detective Kerber from Boston is investigating a murder that happened this past Friday. There might be a connection to your motorhome as well as mine."

He looked at me. "Let's talk about this before we eat dinner. I want to know the details."

I nodded. "I'll tell you everything. But not here. Let's get back to the campsite first. It'll be easier to explain there."

Jean looked at me shaking her head. "You've done it now. He's in detective mode. It'll be hard to get him to do anything else. But if this does involve you and the police, Jack's the man you want on your side."

He was ahead of us, leading the way. "Come on you two, can't you walk any faster?"

Jean looked at me. "I warned you."

Chapter 42

When we got to my campsite, I heard Bob crying at the window. Jean heard him too. "Is that the cat I've been hearing so much about?"

"Yeah, that's him. It sounds like he's out of food or mad that I left him in there alone. I guess I need to go in and check on him before he bothers the other campers."

Jean walked up to the window. "If you don't mind, I'd love to meet him. We had a cat for years, and I still miss her to this day. Maybe he just needs to be held."

I laughed. "Good luck with that. He doesn't seem to be the holding kind of cat. But you're welcome to go in and try. Just be careful when you open the door. I don't want him to get out.

"His name is Bob. Mango Bob. Before you open the door, I'll go over to the driver's side and try to get his attention. When you hear me tap on it, open the door and go in."

I unlocked the side door and ran over to the driver's door and tapped on it to get Bob's attention. Jean heard me tapping and quickly went in the side door. Bob wasn't waiting at either door. He was still at the window above the couch watching the squirrels. He didn't try to escape when Jean went in.

As soon as he saw her, he quieted down. He didn't know what to think. Another stranger had been introduced into his life. I figured he'd run and hide because that's what cats do.

He did get down from the window but apparently didn't run off. We could hear Jean talking to him in a soothing voice, saying his name over and over.

Jack smiled. "She loves cats. After hers passed away, I promised to get her another one. But I never did. I always came up with an excuse about why it just wasn't the right time.

"Spending a little time with yours might be good for her."

I started to remind him that Bob wasn't my cat. I was his chauffeur, taking him to Englewood. But before I could get the words out, he said, "Tell me why you think you're involved in a Boston murder investigation. Start at the beginning. Don't leave anything out."

He took a seat on the concrete bench by the picnic table and I sat across from him. "Here's the story. The company I worked for was liquidating its inventory. One of the things they needed to sell was the motorhome.

"Molly, the human resources manager, asked if I'd be interested in buying it. I wasn't sure I wanted it, but she convinced me that I did, and we eventually worked out a deal.

"The day I bought it, Molly got a call from Harvey Tucker. He worked at corporate headquarters in Boston and wanted to know if the motorhome had been sold.

"When she told him it had, he asked if she knew where it was parked. He mentioned he may have left something in it and wanted to get it.

"Molly told him I was the one who bought it and that I was camping at Toad Suck. She asked if he wanted my phone number. He said no.

"That night, your motorhome, which looks exactly like mine, was broken into. The next day, which was Friday, Tucker called Molly again. He wanted to know exactly where the motorhome was.

"She'd already told me about his first call, and I had asked her to tell him I was on the road and not tell him where I was

186

going.

"The next morning, which was Saturday, Molly got a call from Tim Kerber, a Boston detective. He told her that Tucker had been murdered the night before and they were checking his recent calls.

"That's all I know."

Jack was silent for a moment then asked, "Did you speak to anyone in Boston?"

"No, I only spoke with Molly. She's the one who arranged to sell me the motorhome. She's also the sister of the woman I'm taking Bob to, in Englewood."

Clearly in detective mode, Jack said, "I have to ask this. Are you telling me everything? Is there anything you've left out?"

I hesitated then said, "There is one more thing.

"Yesterday, when driving through Mississippi, two guys tried to carjack me. They waved me over, pulled a gun and tried to take the motorhome."

Jack interrupted me. "Wait. Are you telling me that you were held at gunpoint while driving down here? And you didn't mention it before?"

"No, I didn't say anything because I promised Mavis, the grandmother who was riding with me, that I'd keep it a secret."

"And why is that? Why did she want to keep it a secret?"

I hesitated, wondering how much I should tell him. After thinking about it, I decided he should know everything.

"While the guy held me at gunpoint, his partner went over to the RV, looking for the keys. Mavis, the woman who was riding with me, saw him coming and when he opened the door, she tazed him.

187

"The guy dropped to the ground, and I disarmed the gunman. We put them in the trunk of their car. I called nine one one and we left.

"Mavis didn't want her son, a deputy sheriff, to find out about what had gone down. She made me promise not to tell anyone about it."

Jack thought for a minute. "So someone tries to break into my motorhome Thursday night. Then someone tries to steal yours on Saturday, and, in between, the last person to drive yours is murdered?"

He looked at me, then at my motorhome, then back at me.

"Walker, is there anything in your RV you don't want me to see or know about?"

"No, why?"

"Because I think it might be a good idea to search it to make sure there isn't something in it related to all this—the break-in, the carjacking, and Tucker's murder.

"Before we do anything, I want to call a friend in Boston and see what I can find out.

"I want to be straight with you before I dig into this. If you're involved in criminal activity or are on the run from the law or have warrants, I'm going to turn you in. Understand?"

"Yeah, I understand. But you're not going to find anything. I'm squeaky clean. Never even had a parking ticket."

He smiled the way detectives sometimes do. "So you wouldn't mind showing me your driver's license so I could do a background check?"

"Jack, I have nothing to hide. My driver's license is inside. I'll get it for you."

I walked to the front of the motorhome and looked through the windshield to see if I could locate Bob.

Jean was sitting on the floor and he was in her lap. She was petting him slowly, and even from outside I could hear him purring.

I moved to the driver's door, slowly opened it, reached in and got my wallet.

Hearing me, Jean looked up. "Is Jack in detective mode?"

"Yeah, full bore. But I don't mind. I appreciate his help."

I gently closed the door, not wanting to disturb either of them and walked back to Jack.

"Here's my license. If it would help, I've got an insurance card with the RV's VIN on it."

He smiled. "Most people don't give up their driver's license so easily. I appreciate it. Having the VIN will help."

I gave him the insurance card.

He pointed over his shoulder. "My phone is back in my rig. You stay here with Jean. I'm going to make a few calls. I'll be back in ten minutes."

He took off. A man on a mission.

I stayed outside, listening to his wife tell Bob what a good kitty he was.

Chapter 43

From inside the coach, Jean asked, "What's the story with Bob's tail?"

I only knew what Molly had told me. She hadn't said much, but she had mentioned his tail or lack of it.

"I was told he was born that way. With just a stub of a tail. He doesn't seem to miss it. From the way he acts when he's cornered, he might be part bobcat."

From inside, Jean said, "He sure is a good-looking boy. Big too. He must weigh around twenty-five pounds."

"Yeah, he's big alright. Like a small dog. But with sharp claws."

Again, from inside, "Has he been any trouble?"

"No, not really. He likes to sound off in the middle of the night before he uses his box. But other than that, he's been pretty good."

"Well, he sure likes being petted. He's in here purring up a storm."

She was right. Mango Bob was turning out to be a pretty good cat. Except for the one time he tried to escape. But he was new then and didn't know where he was. Being on the road with a stranger in a moving house scared him. He did what he thought he needed to do. Run.

After he learned that being in the RV meant food, water and litter, along with a soft bed, he'd mellowed a bit. At least that's what I hoped.

Jack returned ten minutes later, talking to someone on his phone. "Yeah, I know. Office politics. Okay, if I find out anything here, I'll let you know."

He came over to me. "Boston says the murder looks like a professional hit. No prints, no shell casings, no sign of forced entry.

"Right now, they don't know if there is a connection between the murder and your motorhome. All they know is Tucker seemed to be very interested in it the day before he was killed.

"Their budget doesn't allow them to send someone down here to check things out. Even if it did, there's no probable cause to get a search warrant.

"So as far as they're concerned, the motorhome is not related to the murder. But I'm not buying it. Someone tried to break into my rig, which looks exactly like yours, and then someone tried to steal yours the next day. Something is definitely going on.

"Somebody is looking for something. They think it is in your RV. That's why they tried to break into mine. They didn't find whatever it was, only because they were looking in the wrong one.

"When that didn't work out, they sent muscle with guns to get the right one. Yours. Because a little old lady had a Taser, they failed.

"So whatever they want, it's probably still in there. And they probably still want it."

I nodded. "So what do we do?"

He handed me back my license and insurance card. "You checked out clean. No record, no warrants, nothing. Interesting military service though. Awarded a few medals, got out with an honorable discharge."

I shrugged.

"The motorhome also checked out. Registered in your name. No liens against it."

He pointed at the Love Bus. "If this were my investigation, I'd get a warrant and search your rig, starting with that locked door we found in the utility compartment.

"But since I'm no longer a detective, and since Boston PD hasn't linked your coach to the murder, there won't be a search warrant."

He paused, waiting for me to say something. I didn't make him wait long.

"You don't need a warrant. I give you permission to search. Just promise you won't let Bob get out. If he escapes, I'll be in big trouble."

He smiled. "Don't worry about the cat. We'll get Jean to babysit him while we do our search. If my hunch is right, we won't need to go inside where the cat is. We'll probably find what we're looking for in that outside compartment."

He rubbed his hands. "Before we get started, we're going to need a flashlight, some Ziploc bags, and plastic gloves. I'm guessing you don't have any of those things with you?"

I laughed. "I've got a flashlight. That's about it."

"That's okay. I've got baggies and gloves in my coach. I'll let Jean know what's going on and then go get my kit."

He spoke to Jean through the open window. "I'm going to get a few things, be right back."

She raised her voice. "Just hold on there, buster. What about dinner? I'm getting hungry. Walker is probably hungry too. Don't leave me here starving while you play detective!"

He sighed. "What if I bring back some TV dinners? We can cook them here, if that's okay with Walker."

I nodded. "Yeah, that works for me. But all I've got is bottled water. If you want something stronger, you'll have to bring it."

193

"Water is fine. I'll be right back."

As he walked away, Jean said, "See what I mean by detective mode? He gets his mind focused on solving a crime and everything else takes second place. I hope we're not imposing by eating in your coach."

"Not at all. I enjoy your company. It looks like Bob is enjoying it as well."

Jean was still stroking his back. "He's a real sweetie. He likes it when I rub his ears. He even let me rub his belly. I think he'd let me do it all night long."

"Yeah, if I could find someone to rub my belly, I might let them do it all night too."

She laughed. "That's the kind of thinking that can get you into woman trouble. Just ask Bob."

Chapter 44

Jack returned with his crime-fighting kit in one hand, a shopping bag full of food in the other.

Jean saw him and said, "Food! Finally! Hand it to me, I'll get it ready."

As she prepared our dinner, Jack and I went to the utility compartment on the backside of the coach and unlocked it.

He pulled on a pair of plastic gloves, picked up a small flashlight, and aimed it at the mystery door inside the compartment.

"That shouldn't be there. Someone added it after the coach left the factory."

He was still looking at the mystery door when Jean announced, "Dinner is ready!"

He looked at me shaking his head. "If there's one thing I've learned in thirty-five years of marriage it's not to ignore a dinner call. Let's go eat."

From outside, I asked Jean, "Is it safe to come in? I don't want Bob getting out."

"Don't worry about him. I've got him under control. Come on in."

We did as we were told. Dinner was on the table. Bob was in the back purring on the bed.

As soon as we sat, Jean pointed at Jack. "Just one rule. No talking about crime while we're eating."

He nodded. "Agreed."

During the meal, we talked about Bob, the drive down, our RVs, the weather, and the price of gas.

I could tell Jack was distracted. He wanted to see what was behind the locked door in the back compartment of my RV.

I did too.

Chapter 45

We'd finished our meals and Jack was fidgeting at the table. He kept looking around the coach, taking it all in. CSI mode.

It was obvious he wanted to go outside and resume his investigation but he wasn't going to do so without Jean's permission.

She laughed. "Oh, go on. It's killing you to have to sit here while there's something to investigate."

He didn't wait to be told twice. He was up and heading for the door before she could say, "Watch out for Bob! Don't let him out!"

It didn't matter. Jack and I were both outside before Bob even knew the door had been opened.

At the back of the coach, Jack had me shine the flashlight on the mystery compartment. He donned his plastic gloves again and said, "Let's try your keys. One of them might work."

The first three keys wouldn't fit. But the fourth one slipped into the lock and turned the cylinder. The compartment popped open.

Inside, we could see what looked like a white washcloth wrapped around a small object, held secure by two rubber bands.

"We need to get video of this. You want to use your phone or mine?" Jack asked.

"Mine. I know how to use it. Might not be able to figure yours out."

I put my phone in video mode and aimed it at the small

compartment door.

"Okay, I'm recording."

Jack started speaking. "I'm Jack Daniels, and today is October 15, 2017. I have been authorized by the owner of this vehicle, John Walker, to search this compartment.

"We have unlocked it and have found an item that appears to be wrapped in a white cloth. I will now reach in and remove it."

He pointed at the mystery object and I moved in for a close-up shot.

He continued. "This is what we found. The current owner of this vehicle has indicated he did not place the object in this compartment.

"I will remove the two rubber bands and unwrap the cloth to see what it is."

He carefully slipped off the two bands and placed them in one of the Ziploc bags he had brought with him.

With the phone still recording, he unwrapped the cloth to reveal a small camera enclosed in a plastic case.

He placed the cloth into another Ziploc bag. "As you can see, we've found what looks to be a small camera. There's a logo on the front that says, 'Hero.' The one on the back says, 'GoPro.'"

He turned it to show the side. "On the side of the camera, there appears to be a memory card slot with a memory card in it."

He looked at me and said, "Okay, you can stop recording now."

He pointed to the camera. "You know what that is, don't you?

"Yeah, it's a GoPro. One of the better pocket-sized action

cams. You see them everywhere these days."

He looked at me. "Wonder why it's hidden back here. Think anything's on it?"

I shrugged. "Might be. I can put the memory card in my laptop and we can find out."

He nodded. "Your laptop inside?"

"Yeah, you want to take a look?"

"You bet I do."

We went back inside and showed Jean what we'd found.

Her eyes lit up. "Really? You found a hidden camera? That's pretty exciting. Think there's anything on it?"

Jack smiled. "We're about to find out."

I went back to the bedroom and got my laptop out of the closet. When I returned, Jack was still wearing plastic gloves and holding the GoPro in his right hand.

He said. "Record me while I do this."

I started the video app on my phone and recorded as he popped opened the waterproof case around the camera. He put the case in one of his Ziploc bags.

Holding the naked GoPro in his hand, he turned it so the memory card slot was in my camera's view.

Using his gloved hand, he gently tapped the back of memory card and it popped out of the slot.

He removed the tiny card and held it up.

"Can your laptop read cards this size?"

I pointed to an opening on the side of the laptop. "Yeah. Just slide the card into that slot."

Jack pushed the card into the card reader. I pointed the phone at the computer to record the screen activity.

A small window popped up saying a removable storage device had been added. That was a good sign. It meant the card wasn't corrupted.

Jack looked at me. "Let me record the video while you operate the computer."

He took my phone and pointed it at the laptop screen while I used the mouse to click on the memory card icon.

A file window opened. No files were listed.

"Jack, we may be out of luck. It doesn't look like there is anything on the card. Either the camera hasn't been used or the files have been erased."

He frowned. "So there's no video on it?"

I shook my head. "Not that we can easily get to. But if the files have been erased, we might be able to recover them."

Back in my job as IT manager, I had lot of experience recovering lost or damaged files. With the right software, it could usually be done. I happened to have the needed software on my laptop.

"Jack, I've got something that should be able to recover files recently deleted from the card. You want me to give it a try?"

He thought a moment then asked, "Will it alter or change the contents of the memory card in any way?"

"No. It doesn't change the card. The program looks for deleted files and if any are found it saves them onto the laptop. The file structure on the card isn't touched."

"If you're absolutely sure the memory card won't be altered, do it."

I started the process. In less than a minute, the software announced it had found something.

"Jack, good news. There are four deleted files on the card.

Photos and videos. I'll tell the program to recover them."

It took the app ten long minutes to rebuild the missing files. That meant the files were probably quite large.

When the program finished, I said, "Jack, it's done. We don't need the card anymore. You can take it out."

He removed the memory card and put it back in the GoPro, which he then put in a Ziploc baggie.

Our next step was to find out what was on the files we'd recovered.

Chapter 46

"Jack, the files are date stamped. Let's look at them oldest to newest, see what we have."

"Sounds good. Get started."

I clicked on the first file name.

It opened with a close-up photo of a man's hand reaching toward the camera. You couldn't see his face. Just a closeup of his open palm.

Jack looked at the photo and shook his head. "Can't tell who it is or what they are doing. Show me the next one."

The second file was also a photo. Shot from inside the motorhome from the front, looking toward the back bedroom. There were no people in the shot.

Jack nodded and said, "Show me the next one."

The third file was a video.

It started with a close-up of the same hand we had seen in the first photo. Then the hand pulled back to reveal a man looking directly into the camera.

"Jack, that's Harvey Tucker, the guy who was murdered."

In the video, Tucker took a few steps back and said, "Testing. Testing. Testing."

He moved to the coach door and looked at the camera again. "Testing, testing, testing."

From the coach door, he moved to the dinette table. He smiled at the camera and said, "Testing. Testing. Testing."

Finally, he walked back to the camera, his hand reached toward the lens and the video went black.

Jack nodded. "Looks like he was testing the camera placement. Making sure it picked up whatever he wanted to record.

"Play the next one. Let's see what he was trying to get."

I clicked the file name. It was another video.

It started with a clear shot of the interior of the motorhome. No people in the scene. No movement.

Five minutes into the video, indistinct voices could be heard from outside the coach. As the video continued, the coach door opened and Harvey Tucker stepped into the frame. He was talking to someone behind him, off-camera.

He moved to the dinette table as a second man, tall and bronze-skinned, dressed in a white Panama suit, walked in. He was followed by a shorter, heavy-set man carrying a briefcase.

Tucker spoke first. "This is my little home away from home. We're safe here. No one is around. No one knows we are here. Please, have a seat."

The suited man nodded and sat. The heavy-set man with the briefcase stood behind him, saying nothing.

Tucker spoke to the well-dressed man sitting across from him. "As promised, I was able to get the company to choose your property for the new plant location. Your people have been hired to oversee the construction."

With a heavy accent, the suited man said, "Yes, you delivered on your promise. I will fulfill mine."

He snapped his fingers. The heavy-set man placed the briefcase he'd been holding on the table in front of Tucker. Then he stepped back.

The man in the white suit looked up, unlatched the briefcase and opened it.

"In here, you'll find ten rolls of US Eagle gold coins. Each roll contains twenty coins. Two hundred in all.

"These are now yours."

The suited man continued. "When the equipment from the Conway plant is delivered and installed at our location, I will deliver another two hundred coins."

Tucker reached over and removed one of the rolls from the briefcase. He appeared surprised at the weight.

He put the roll back in place, closed the briefcase, snapped the locks shut, and placed it under the table.

He smiled and reached out to shake the hand of the suited man. "It is a pleasure doing business with you. You are a man of your word."

The suited man replied, "I expect you to ensure the movement and installation of the manufacturing equipment goes smoothly.

"If it goes as planned, we will meet again and complete our business."

The suited man stood. "I must go now. My flight departs soon."

He took two steps toward the door then turned back to face Tucker. "Do not think because I am pleasant to deal with that there will not be consequences should things not turn out well.

"Should our arrangement be revealed to others, or should it not be completed to my satisfaction, much harm will come to you.

"Do you understand this?"

Tucker nervously stood. "Yes, I understand. But there's nothing to worry about. Our arrangement is completely confidential. It will go as planned."

"Make sure it does. Life will be much more pleasant for you if nothing goes wrong."

With that, the heavy-set man opened the door and stepped out. The suited man paused until the large man stepped back into the camera view and nodded his head.

The suited man then stepped out of the door and walked out of the camera view.

Tucker sat down and said nothing.

He appeared to be listening. Off-camera a car door closed. Then another. The car started, and gravel crunched as it drove off.

Tucker remained motionless for another minute.

Then he stood, walked toward the camera, reached up, and the video ended.

Chapter 47

I had a hard time believing what I had just seen on the video. But it had happened. "That son of a bitch! He took a payoff to close the plant. Six hundred people are out of work because of him."

Jack nodded. "That's what it looks like. And the people he dealt with didn't want anyone to know about it."

"You're right. But why would they kill him? He kept his end of the deal. The plant's been closed and the equipment's been shipped south."

Jack shook his head. "We don't know if these people killed him. Could have been someone else. But I doubt it. By accepting that payment, he became a liability to them. If they let him live, he'd always be a threat."

"If they killed him, they wouldn't have to pay him the rest of the gold. They might even be able to recover what they'd already given him.

"Maybe Tucker recorded the video as insurance. Or as a way to get more money. That's probably why he was trying to find the motorhome. To get the camera. But why leave it here in the first place? Why not take it and hide it somewhere safer?"

It was a good question. Then I remembered what Molly had said.

"He planned to buy the motorhome. That's why he left the camera in it. He figured it was a safe place to hide it.

"But when corporate tried to contact him to close the sale, he was nowhere to be found. That's why they sold it to me. They couldn't find Tucker."

It made sense. Except for one thing.

"The files had been erased. So why would he worry about the camera?"

Jack thought about it. "Maybe he didn't want someone accidentally finding it. It was easy for you to recover the files. Someone else could have done the same thing.

"A more important question is did Tucker hire someone to break into the motorhome to get the camera or did the man in the suit learn about the video and send someone after it?"

Neither of us knew the answer. But we knew the video was important.

Jack stood. "I need to let Boston PD know about this and send them a copy. I'll call my contact there and let them know what we found.

"They'll probably want me to send the camera, the card, everything. They'll be able to recover the video files the same way you did, right?"

"Yeah, they should be able to. But just in case, I'll make a copy of all the files and give them to you. That way, we'll all have copies."

I paused then asked, "Once Boston gets the video, I should be completely out of this, right?"

Jack looked up and shook his head. "Probably not.

"Since this looks like a crime that crosses international borders, the FBI might get involved. That means they'll want a copy of the video and they may want to talk to you."

I didn't like the sound of that. I didn't want to be tied to a federal investigation that might drag on for years. I didn't want my name mixed up in it. I didn't want the bad guys knowing who I was or where I was living.

But the news from Jack got worse.

"Whoever was looking for the camera might still be looking for it. They might try to track you down."

That was the last thing I wanted to hear. That someone might be still trying to find me and my RV. As long as they were out there, I'd have to be looking over my shoulder, wondering when they would strike. It wasn't the kind of life I'd envisioned when I bought the RV and headed to Florida.

Jack could see I was worried. "Here's what we can do. I'll call my contact in Boston and let him know what's on the video.

"He'll probably want me to send a copy to the FBI. Once word gets out that the FBI has the video, whoever was looking for it, will no longer have a reason to come after you or the RV. We'll just have to make sure the word gets out."

"That'll happen pretty quickly when Boston PD and the Feds start interviewing people about what's on the video.

"They may have a few questions for you, too. I'll have them go through me.

"Jean and I will be in Venice, just a few miles north of Englewood where you're going. We'll stay in touch."

He took a business card from his wallet, wrote his cell number on the back and handed it to me.

Jean had sat quietly while we watched the video and discussed what it might mean. Finally she spoke up. "Don't wait for something to come up to call us. After you get settled in Englewood, call. Let us know what you're doing, where you're staying.

"If Bob ever needs a cat-sitter, let me know. I'll be happy to take him in."

Jack stood to leave. "Let's get together in the morning. Say about eight o'clock?"

I nodded. "Sounds good to me. You fixing breakfast for all of us?"

"No, but the campground cafe should be open by then. I'll meet you there."

Jean gave me a hug. "Don't worry about this. It'll be okay. Jack's got your back."

They both left for the night, leaving me and Bob wondering what was going to happen next.

Chapter 48

My phone alarm chimed me awake.

The windows were still open from the night before. Wildlife was stirring outside. Other campers were getting ready to leave. Bob was sleeping at the foot of the bed.

The clock showed I had about an hour before I needed to meet Jack. More than enough time to shower and shave.

I hadn't bothered to hook up to campground water; it was less of a hassle to walk to the campground bathhouse and shower there. I grabbed a towel, soap, shampoo, and headed out.

The showers weren't crowded. The water was warm.

When I got back to the coach, Bob was at the window keeping watch over two squirrels playing tag in a nearby tree. He looked at me over his shoulder and said, "Murrph," telling me he could get those squirrels if he wanted to.

I was sure he could.

I powered up my laptop and checked my email. I found a lot of spam but nothing important.

I googled "Harvey Tucker" to see if anything about his case had made the news.

It had.

There was an article in the *Boston Globe* about his murder. It said he had resigned from his job the week before his death. Something about an investigation of "improprieties" at work.

I wondered if it involved his south of the border dealings? Did someone find out? Was that why he was killed?

The article didn't get into it. It just said he was murdered and it looked like a professional hit. The police weren't releasing any details other than saying it was an ongoing investigation.

After reading the article, I checked the weather for Englewood. The forecast was for blue skies and low humidity. A gentle breeze off the gulf. Perfect weather for traveling in an RV.

When it was time to meet Jack for breakfast, I checked on Bob. He was still on squirrel patrol at the window.

I headed out, locking the door behind me.

The campground cafe was in the open plaza overlooking the springs. It took me about three minutes to get there. Jack was waiting. He smiled and said, "I wondered if you were going to sleep in this morning. Have a good night?"

"Yeah, not bad. Bob woke me about three in the morning to let me know he was going to use his litter box. He was quiet after that."

Jack laughed. "At least he uses the box. With our cat, I took too long to clean her box once. She repaid me by pooping in my shoe. I learned to keep her litter clean after that."

"Yeah, they do like a clean box. But so far, I really can't complain about Bob. He's been pretty easy to live with."

Jack looked toward the springs. "You up for a walk before breakfast?"

"I'm always up for a walk."

We followed the signs to the nature trail and decided to do the four-mile loop to the sinkhole and back.

While we were walking, Jack said, "I called Boston again this morning. Talked to the lead detective on the Tucker case.

"He said until they see the video, they won't know if it's important or not.

"He said even if the video shows a bribe, the Boston PD won't pursue it. Bribery is a class E felony. Even if convicted, it's only minimal jail time. Since the person who accepted the bribe is dead, there's not much of a case.

"He also said their investigators didn't find any gold coins in Tucker's apartment. He either hid them or cashed them in. Either way, it's not something Boston PD is worried about.

"As it stands now, they say you're out of it. In the clear."

"Good. I don't want to be involved in a murder investigation.

"Can I tell Molly? She's the person who sold me the motorhome and took the calls from Tucker. She's pretty worried about the whole thing."

"No, don't tell her anything. Let her hear it from the Boston PD. It'll be better that way."

We continued our walk, marveling at the great Florida weather and all the wildlife in the park.

If it was any indication of what living in Florida was going to be like, sign me up for more.

We eventually got back to the park cafe and ordered breakfast. Eggs, toast, sausage and orange juice.

"Where's Jean this morning? I thought she might be joining us."

Jack smiled. "She said she wanted to sleep in. But I'm guessing she just wanted to give us some time to talk about the case without her being around."

I nodded. "So Jack, what's the best way to get from here to Englewood?"

He used a paper napkin to draw the route. "Stay on 19

213

until you get to Crystal River. Then get on I-75 and stay on it all the way to the Englewood exit. Expect heavy traffic around Tampa, but unless you go through during rush hour, it shouldn't be too bad.

"It'll take you about five hours to get to Englewood, assuming no major traffic tie-ups on 75."

He stood. "Jean and I will be leaving in about half an hour. We probably won't see you again on this trip. Call me if anything comes up. Or just call if you get bored. Either way, stay in touch.

"Don't leave without saying goodbye to Jean."

We finished our breakfast and headed back to our campsites. Jack's was closest and as we approached, Jean came out of the motorhome. "Don't you dare leave without giving me a hug!"

She walked up and gave me a big squeeze then said, "I don't know if Jack told you, but meeting you has made this trip one of our best. Jack got to play detective and I got to play with Bob.

"We'll be in Venice, which is only about eight miles north of Englewood. After you get settled in, give us a call and we'll get together.

"Promise you'll let us know if anything comes up. Or if you just need someone to talk to. We'll have plenty of time on our hands, and we'd love to hear from you."

I nodded. "I've got both your phone numbers and email addresses, I promise to stay in touch."

With that, she hugged me again, Jack shook my hand, and I headed back to my campsite thinking about how lucky I had been to meet them both.

Chapter 49

When I got back to the Love Bus, I programmed the route Jack had suggested into my GPS. I checked on Bob and started getting things ready for the road.

After closing all the windows, I went back outside, disconnected from shore power, and made sure the utility compartment was tidy and locked. I took a final walk around the coach to make sure I hadn't forgotten anything.

Bob watched with interest from his perch on the back of the couch. The last thing on my list before hitting the road was to call Molly's sister in Englewood and let her know I'd be getting there later that day.

I dug through my wallet and found the business card Molly had given me. Her sister's name was Sarah and she worked at Dolphin Adventure Tours on Mango Street in Old Englewood, Florida.

I dialed the number. After four rings a woman answered. "Dolphin Adventure Tours, how can I help you?"

"Sarah?"

"No, Sarah is out on the water this morning. I'm Becky."

"Becky, I'm Walker. I've got Sarah's cat. I'll be in Englewood this afternoon."

"That's great! Sarah said she was hoping you'd be here today. She told me to tell you to park out on the street. Don't pull into the driveway.

"If she's not back when you get here, hang around till she returns. She has a morning and an afternoon tour today and she should be back around four-thirty.

"She's really excited about you bringing her cat. She's been

215

talking about it all weekend."

"That's good to know.

"Becky, I'm kind of new at driving a motorhome and want to avoid heavy city traffic. Will I have any problem getting into Englewood or finding parking?"

She laughed. "You've never been here, have you? Englewood is a small town of about sixteen thousand people. Most of them live on the other side of the county.

"There won't be much traffic no matter what time of day you get here. You won't have any problem parking in front of our office. Just be careful on I-75. It gets crazy during rush hour.

"Once you get on Old Englewood Road, things slow way down. In fact, you're likely to see more people riding bikes than driving cars.

"If you run into any problems, give me a call. I'm Sarah's answering service and live a few doors down from her office."

I thanked her for her help and said I'd probably be there around three.

We said our goodbyes and disconnected. It was time to drive the final leg of my trip south.

I started the coach, let the motor warm up for a few minutes, rechecked all the doors and windows, then pulled out of the campsite.

It took about fifteen minutes to get from the campground back to highway 19. Then a two-hour drive to Crystal River where I took the ramp onto I-75.

Driving on the interstate was far different than the slow, unhurried pace of the back roads I'd been on earlier. The speed limit was seventy, but most everyone was doing at least seventy-five. Some were going a lot faster.

I didn't try to keep up with them. I kept the motorhome in the right lane, set the cruise control to sixty-five, and just ignored those who sped by.

As Jack had predicted, it took three hours to reach the Englewood exit. Due to the traffic and crazy drivers, they were the most stressful three hours of the entire trip.

Taking the Englewood exit, I left the craziness of I-75 behind and found myself on a two-lane road bordered by palm trees and rolling pastures.

Tropical birds flew between the trees, and white sand hinted of the nearby beaches.

The area was more like what I was expecting to see in Florida.

Chapter 50

I followed the two-lane road into Englewood. There was almost no traffic and no signs of civilization other than the surprisingly well-kept road.

Eventually, I came to a sign welcoming me to town. The cow pastures I had passed on the way in gave way to the lifeblood of small towns everywhere. A church, a post office, a grocery store, and, further in, a row of small well-kept homes.

At the first stoplight, the sign said the road to the left led south to Port Charlotte and Punta Gorda. The road to the right led to Venice. Straight ahead would take me to Old Englewood Village on Dearborn Street.

The GPS said to go straight for two hundred yards then turn left onto Mango.

Almost as soon as I turned onto Mango, the GPS told me I had reached my destination. But it had to be a mistake. There was no Dolphin Tours sign.

The La Stanza restaurant was on one side of the street and the Mango Bistro was on the other. Neither was what I was looking for.

But further down the street, just beyond an overgrown lot, I saw a faded sign with the words Dolphin Adventure Tours painted in white.

I drove up to the sign and parked in front of an old block building. I got out and went up to the door. There was a note that said, "We'll be back at four."

I was an hour early. I would have to wait to meet Sarah.

I went back to the motorhome and checked on Bob. He

was sleeping on the bed, with a paw over his eyes.

He didn't know it yet, but he was home. His days of riding shotgun in the Love Bus were over. My days of living in a house on wheels were just getting started.

Chapter 51

Forty minutes later, a white Toyota Tacoma pickup that looked a lot like the one I had just sold came down Mango towing a trailer with eight kayaks on the back. It pulled to the curb in front of me.

A woman was driving. Sarah.

She stepped out and waved. I waved back.

She was about five foot four. Wearing a bright orange fishing shirt, faded cargo shorts and tennis shoes. Her head was covered with a dark blue ball cap. A faded blonde ponytail poked out the back.

She started walking toward the Love Bus and I stepped out to greet her. "You must be Sarah."

"Yeah, and you must be Walker. Is Bob in there?"

"He is. Sleeping in the back."

"Good. Let's not wake him.

She pointed back to her truck. "I need to get these boats into the yard. Give me a hand."

"Okay, what do you need me to do?"

"I'm going to pull the truck into the boatyard; when I get it turned around, you can help me unload it."

She went to her truck, started it up and pulled forward into the driveway next to the Dolphin Tours building. An ivy-covered chain link fence blocked her way. A gate separated the lot behind the fence from the street. Sarah opened it and pulled her truck into the gravel parking area behind the building. After the trailer cleared the gate, she stopped and got out of her truck.

She looked over at me and said, "Don't just stand there. Give me a hand. I've been doing kayak tours all day. Got to wash the boats down to get the sand and salt off them. You can help."

She walked to the trailer tongue, lifted it up off the truck's hitch, and started pulling it toward the corner of the lot.

"You going to just stand there while I move this trailer by myself?"

I laughed. "I was enjoying the show. But since you asked so nicely, what can I do to help?"

"Grab the front of the trailer and pull it over there by the wall. By the water hose."

I picked up the tongue of the trailer. It wasn't heavy, which was good. It would have been bad if I couldn't have handled it as easily as Sarah had.

I pulled it over to the wall, stopping when she said, "That's good. Now stand back while I hose the boats down."

I got out of her way and watched as she sprayed the salt and sand off each boat. After she finished, she threw a wet sponge in my direction and said, "Time to wipe them down."

She dipped her sponge in a bucket of soapy water and went to work. I did the same. We cleaned each boat. When we were finished, she sprayed them down again.

Finally, she said, "That's good enough."

She wiped her hands on her pants, then reached out to me. "Let's start over. I'm Sarah."

I shook her hand and said, "Just call me Walker."

"Okay. Walker it is."

She pointed over her shoulder. "Everything in the fenced-in area is part of the old boatyard. I rent it and the building next door.

"Back when it was a boatyard, they had a night watchman who lived in an Airstream trailer over there in the corner. He and the trailer are both long gone. The power, water, and sewer connection are still there.

"You can park your motorhome there for the time being. But before you do, you have to agree to my rules. If you don't like them, you can go somewhere else."

"Okay, tell me what they are."

She put her hands on her hips and started in. "No smoking or drinking. No drugs. No visitors. No loud music. The gate has to be closed and locked at all times. You can't do anything to call attention to being camped back here."

She paused, apparently waiting for me to say something.

I answered quickly.

"No problem. I can live with that."

"Good, with one more condition. If I say it's time for you to pack up and go, you go. No argument. Understood?"

"Yeah, I got it."

"It's nothing personal. But I don't know anything about you. You might be the greatest guy in the world. Or just another loser I don't need hanging around.

"It's better to get the rules straight before we go any further."

She was right. I was a stranger and she was inviting me into her life. For all she knew, I could be the worst thing that ever happened to her. The rules gave her an out.

"I understand completely. Having rules will make it easier for both of us."

She relaxed. "Now that we have that out of the way, let's get your RV in here.

"Pull in through the gate and back it up into the far corner over there. That's where the trailer hookups are."

Without waiting for me to say anything, she walked to her truck and moved it out of the way so I could pull in.

I came in slowly, being careful not to hit anything. After I got the RV turned around, I lined it up with the chain link fence and started backing up.

She guided me in. "To the right, okay, come on. Slow, slow. Stop.

"That's good. Perfect."

I put it in park and shut down the motor. I stepped out of the driver's door and walked over to Sarah.

She smiled. "Looks good. The neighbors will never know it's there."

Apparently it would have been a problem if they did. Knowing that, I'd do my best not to do anything that might rile them up.

"Sarah, I really appreciate you letting me park here. I'm happy to pay."

She shook her head. "Nope, you're not going to pay me anything. But I might ask you to help with a few chores."

I smiled. "Whatever you want; just let me know."

I figured the next thing she'd say would be about the cat. I'd brought him a long way and thought she'd want to see him. But I was wrong. Instead of asking about Bob, she said, "I bet after being on the road you'd like a home-cooked meal."

"Yeah, that sounds pretty good."

"It sounds good to me too. But I don't cook. So we're going to eat out tonight."

"Fine with me, as long as you drive."

"No problem. I don't mind driving, but you're buying."

I smiled. "You pick the spot, and I'll pick up the tab."

There were a few moments of awkward silence. I broke it by asking, "Are you ready for Bob?"

She shook her head. "No, not yet. I need to set up a space for him inside. Before I do that, I want to go in, take a shower and get into some clean clothes."

She pointed at the building in front of us. "I live in the back of the office. That's my private place. It's off-limits to you.

"I'll meet you back out here around five.

"While I'm inside, close the gate and do whatever you need to do to hook up your motorhome.

"See you at five."

She went in the building's side door, leaving me alone in the yard.

Chapter 52

After closing the gate, I walked back to the Love Bus. Looking around behind it, I found the water spigot and power connections the old Airstream had used. I hooked up to both. There was a sewer connection, but I didn't bother with it. I'd leave that for another day.

Inside, I checked on Bob. He was still sleeping and hadn't touched his food since earlier that morning. That seemed to be his daily routine. Prowl at night, sleep late in the morning, eat after getting up, and then sleep all day. Most humans would be jealous of that kind of life.

I sure was.

As I started thinking about what I would wear for dinner, my phone chimed with a call from Molly.

"Hi, what's up?"

"Walker, just checking to see if you made it to Sarah's yet."

"I have. I got here a few minutes ago. Met her and helped her wash down her boats."

"So Walker, what do you think?"

"About what?"

"Sarah. What do you think about Sarah?"

I laughed. "Molly, I just met her a few minutes ago. What am I supposed to think? She's nice-looking and likes to take charge. She gave me a set of rules I have to abide by or else. Other than that, I can't tell you much."

"So you think she's good-looking?"

"Molly, I'm not going to talk to you about your sister's looks. I've just met her and, besides, why are you so interested in what I think about her? Are you trying to set us up?"

"No, nothing like that. It's just that you and her have a lot in common. You'd be good for each other."

"Molly, I've only been here twenty minutes. I just met your sister and other than listening to her tell me the rules, we haven't talked. So no, we haven't decided to get married and have children."

She sighed. "Okay, enough about Sarah. Did the Boston PD talk to you about Tucker's murder?"

I had to be careful with my answer. I didn't want to tell her the full story. Not yet anyway.

"No, I haven't spoken to anyone in Boston. I did read in the paper that Tucker was fired two weeks ago. When he called you on Thursday, he was no longer employed by the company. I don't know whether he was fired or quit or why he was so interested in the Love Bus. I guess we'll just have to wait and see what the police find out."

"Yeah, I guess we will. What about you? Now that you're in Florida, what are your plans?"

"Molly, I just got here and my plans are to stay at your sister's place for a few days while I figure things out. Right now my most pressing decision is what to wear this evening when I go to dinner with her."

She squealed. "You have a date with Sarah? Already? Woohoo!"

"Bye, Molly." I sighed and hung up.

Chapter 53

Choosing what to wear for my dinner date with Sarah was pretty easy. Mainly because my choices were limited to the few clothes I hadn't boxed up and stored in the basement of the coach.

The only things in my closet were two pair of jeans, two long-sleeve shirts, a sweater, and a jacket. Fine for Arkansas winters but not so much for sunny Florida.

I washed up, chose the least wrinkled shirt, matched it with the freshest jeans, and called myself good to go.

I had about thirty minutes before I needed to meet up with Sarah, so I decided to check to see what local stations were available on the TV.

After cranking up the antenna and pushing the amplifier button, I scanned and found fourteen channels. Four from Fort Myers, two from Sarasota and eight from Tampa.

I clicked through them, pausing long enough to catch the local weather. Clear skies, highs in the low seventies, lows in the mid-fifties. No humidity and a slight breeze over the gulf.

You couldn't ask for much better.

I turned the TV off and fired up my computer to check my email. There was nothing important. Just spam.

With time to kill, I brought up Google Maps and entered the Mango Street address where I was parked. Using the satellite view and zooming in, I could see the boatyard and the surrounding area.

Zooming back a bit revealed a large body of water at the end of Dearborn, the street I had driven in on. The map said it was Lemon Bay.

Beyond Lemon Bay was the long, narrow barrier island of Manasota Key and beyond that the Gulf of Mexico.

From where I was parked, it was just a few hundred yards to the beach. I was looking forward to my first few steps in the sand.

From outside I heard footsteps followed by Sarah's voice asking, "Walker? You awake?"

"Yeah, just checking my email."

The sound of her voice woke Bob. He jumped down from the bed, came over to me and said, "Murrfph?"

Sarah didn't hear him. She said, "Let's go. You don't want to keep me waiting when I'm hungry."

Bob hopped up on the couch trying to peek outside. "Murrph?"

This time, she heard him. "Bob, is that you? Is that my Mango Bob?"

I went to the door and said, "You might as well come in and see him. He wants to tell you his story."

She stepped in and walked over to the couch where Bob had been waiting. When she reached out to pet him, he backed away; he wasn't sure who she was. She held her hand out, and he slowly moved in and sniffed it. He then looked up at her, meowed softly, and leaned into her hand. He wanted to be petted.

Sarah sat down on the couch and Bob was soon in her lap. She rubbed his head and said, "Bob, I've missed you so much. You're such a brave kitty. I'm never going to let you go again."

He purred as she stroked his back and rubbed his ears. His tail twitched and he meowed softly every time she said his name.

Eventually, he'd had enough. It was time for his evening

nap. He stood, stretched, and trotted back to the bedroom.

Sarah looked at me, tears in her eyes. "I missed him so much. Thanks for bringing him back to me."

I shrugged. "No problem. I kind of enjoyed having him around. If you ever need someone to take care of him, let me know."

She shook her head. "My loser ex-boyfriend hated cats. I don't know why I ever let him convince me to let Bob go. It was stupid. I should have dumped the boyfriend and kept Bob."

I didn't know what to say, so I kept my mouth shut.

She looked up at me. "You and Bob seem to get along pretty well."

"Yeah, I guess we do. I talk to him; he tells me things. We're tight. Right now, he says he wants to sleep. Maybe it's a good time for that home-cooked meal you promised."

She smiled. "I think you're right. Let's go eat."

I locked the door as we left and made sure I had my wallet so I could pay for dinner.

Outside, Sarah asked, "So where do you want to eat?"

I shrugged. "It's your town; you know all the good places. You decide."

She nodded. "Okay, but you'll have to help. What do you like?"

I thought about it, then said, "I've been trying to get to Florida for three days and have yet to see the ocean or the beach. If you can think of a place where I can see either, I'll be happy."

She smiled. "I know just the place."

Chapter 54

Sarah was driving.

We headed up Dearborn and stopped at the light. When it turned green, we crossed the intersection and turned left into the Publix parking lot. She found a space near the front and parked.

"We're eating at a grocery store?"

Ignoring my question, she stepped out of the truck and said, "Grab a basket and try to keep up."

I followed as she went through the sliding doors and headed to the seafood counter at the back of the store.

The man there said, "Hi Sarah. What's it going to be this evening?"

"Hey Ed. How's the shrimp?"

"Fresh off the boat. How much do you want?"

"Give me a pound and steam it for me, okay?"

"Sure, you want Old Bay?"

"Yeah."

"Will do. It'll be ready in seven minutes."

She turned to me and said, "Follow me."

Since she knew the store layout and I didn't, I followed.

She led me up and down the aisles dropping different things into the basket I was carrying. Shrimp cocktail sauce. Saltine crackers. Cheddar cheese. A fresh lemon. Two plastic drinking cups. A roll of paper towels.

In the liquor aisle, she pointed to the shelves and asked, "You prefer beer or wine?"

Hoping it wasn't a trick question, I said, "I'm not much of a beer drinker. But I do drink a little wine now and then."

"Good. My old boyfriend was a heavy drinker. He'd get sloppy drunk on beer and try to kiss me. It turned me off to the smell. So wine it is."

She picked out a bottle of inexpensive Pinot Grigio. From there, we went back to the seafood counter where our shrimp was ready. She picked it up and put it in the basket I was carrying.

"Okay, this should do it. Let's get out of here."

She headed to the ten items or less checkout line. There was only one person in front of us. Sarah emptied the basket onto the conveyor belt. When the cashier greeted us, Sarah pointed at me and said, "He's paying."

The cashier rang us up and I paid with a credit card.

Sarah was already out the door when I grabbed the two grocery bags full of food and followed her like a well-trained puppy.

After I put the bags in the back seat of her truck, she said, "Buckle up and hold on." And off we went.

We turned left out of the parking lot then took a right at the second stop light. That took us to a draw bridge overlooking a large body of water. Pointing out the window, Sarah said, "That's Lemon Bay, where I do most of my kayak tours."

Crossing the bridge, took us into a different world. Instead of the sleepy feeling of Old Englewood, we were now in a laid-back beach town. Both sides of the road were lined with fishing guides, kayak rentals, seafood cafes and more than one souvenir shop selling sea shells. Unlike other beach towns in Florida, this one didn't seem to have wild crowds, amusement parks, or out-of-control teens.

A half mile beyond the bridge, Sarah pulled into a parking lot and announced, "We're here. Manasota Beach. Grab the food and follow me."

She stepped out of the truck and headed toward a set of wooden stairs leading to a covered boardwalk. With the two grocery bags in hand, I followed. When I reached the top of the stairs, I was amazed at what lay before me.

A sugar-white sandy beach bordering the deep blue waters of the Gulf of Mexico stretching to the horizon. The sound of the surf mixed in with the calls of sea gulls and the smell of salt water filled the air.

I was in heaven. This was what I had expected Florida to be like.

Sarah called out to me, "Quit gawking like a tourist. Bring the food over here."

As instructed, I took the grocery bags to the picnic table where she was sitting. She took the wine out of the largest bag, unscrewed the top and filled two of the cups.

She handed one of them to me and said, "Welcome to Florida."

We toasted and after five minutes of sipping wine and watching the waves roll in, our cups were empty.

Sarah refilled them and said, "We're not supposed to have glass on the beach. If you'll put the bottle back in the truck, I'll have the food ready when you get back."

She tossed me the keys. "Be sure to lock it."

When I got back from her truck, our feast was spread out on one of the wooden picnic tables. Steamed shrimp, cocktail sauce, sliced cheddar cheese, crackers, fresh lemon halves, and wine.

She pointed to the shrimp. "I probably should have asked

you this back at the store. Are you allergic to shellfish?"

I laughed. "No, I'm not. In fact, I love peel and eat 'em shrimp."

"Good. I guess that means you know how it works. I dated a guy once who didn't. He crunched through the shells until I told him he was doing it wrong. He was supposed to peel the shells off, throw them away and eat the shrimp.

"He was pretty embarrassed. Two days later he said I wasn't his type. He claimed I was too bossy."

I didn't say anything.

"What are you smiling about? You think I'm bossy?"

I tried to change the subject. "This is an amazing place. You come here often?"

It didn't work.

"So you do think I'm bossy!"

I carefully thought out my reply. "Sarah, I just met you, and you seem like a person who knows what she wants. You like to lead. Those are excellent traits."

She smiled. "Good save. Now eat."

We piled freshly steamed shrimp onto our paper plates and started our meal.

Sarah was methodical. She would peel the shells off several shrimps then eat them one by one. While peeling, she could carry on a conversation.

I, on the other hand, would peel a single shrimp and eat it. Then peel another. Doing it that way kept me busy and limited my replies to her comments and questions.

As we ate our meal, I took it all in. The sandy beach. The sounds of the surf. The salty breeze off the gulf. The setting sun in the distance.

"This was a good idea. Fresh shrimp on the beach. No crowds, no smoky or noisy bars, and no dishes to clean. I guess you've done this before."

She smiled. "I have, but this is the first time I've brought someone with me. You just seemed like a person who might enjoy it."

I nodded. "I am, and I could get used to it. Eating fresh shrimp at the beach. And hanging out with a bossy woman."

She looked up, smiled devilishly, and threw a shrimp at me.

Chapter 55

After we'd finished our meal, Sarah put the leftover cheese and crackers and plastic cups in a grocery bag and asked me to take them back to the truck.

She put everything else in the nearest waste bin.

When I returned, she asked, "Are you up for a walk on the beach?"

"You bet. Ready whenever you are."

She left the table and went down a set of wooden stairs leading to the beach. I followed.

Out on the sand, she took my hand led me to the water's edge. We stood there for a few moments looking out over the surf.

She gave my hand a squeeze, let it go and started walking along the shoreline. I quickly followed, occasionally stopping to look at seashells.

We walked in silence for what seemed like ten minutes. Maybe more. She finally turned back to me and said, "Let's sit and talk."

Without waiting for my response, she walked to the heel of a dune and sat. I sat beside her. Saying nothing. Just looking at the beach and setting sun. To me this was paradise.

When she finally spoke, she said, "You probably think I'm bossy. And I am.

"But I have to be. I lead four to six kayak tours a week. Most of the people going with me have never seen a kayak. Some can't even swim.

"I learned the hard way. They want me to be their leader,

to tell them what to do when we're out on the water. By being bossy, I protect those people. I keep them out of trouble. I make sure they don't drown. I give orders and they follow them.

"So yeah, I'm in the habit of telling people what to do. Sometimes it spills over into my personal life. I give orders and expect people to follow.

"I think I've been doing that ever since we met this afternoon. I apologize. I'm sorry."

She was being serious.

I didn't know how to respond, but I knew I had to say something. "Sarah, I've enjoyed every minute of your company. And, yes, I can see you are a 'take charge' kind of person. But that doesn't bother me. In fact, it makes my life easier.

"It means I don't have to guess what I should be doing around you. I just do what you tell me. At least, up to a point."

She smiled. "Yep, that's the way it should be. I'll tell you what to do, and you'll do it. But there may be times when I want you to take the lead. To tell me what you want to do. You'll know when."

She stood and walked away, going toward the incoming tide. When she turned and saw I wasn't following, she said, "Come on, you're going to miss the sunset."

I got up and went over to where she was standing. The sun was setting in the distance, a bright red ball slowly dropping down into the ocean. It was calming. Something I needed after what I had been through the past month. I was thankful Sarah had brought me to the beach. And happy to be standing there with her.

Chapter 56

After the sun had fallen below the horizon, we walked to the dunes near the back of the beach and sat again.

"Sarah, I know you and your sister Molly grew up in Arkansas. How did you end up in Florida?"

She laughed. "I met a guy. Kevin. We dated for a few months. Neither of us had a job. We were struggling.

"His parents lived down here. They offered us jobs and a place to stay if we moved here to be close to them.

"I hated leaving Molly, but I was young and in love, and Florida seemed like an adventure.

"We moved down to Bradenton where his parents lived. They had an apartment above their garage, and we moved into it.

"His father was a boat captain and took tourists deep-sea fishing five days a week.

"He offered us jobs as deckhands. Basically we were wait-staff for the tourists. We baited their hooks and cleaned the fish they caught. Whatever they needed.

"Kevin couldn't handle it. He got seasick just about every time we went out.

"He quit, but I stayed on. I liked being on the water, and I liked dealing with people.

"After two months, he and I broke up. I had to move out of the garage apartment, but I kept working for his father for two more years.

"Then he sold his boat to a guy in Englewood. Captain Frank. He asked if I wanted to stay on as a deckhand. I did and moved to Englewood to be closer to the boat.

"Captain Frank liked me and taught me everything I needed to know about the business. He even helped me get a six-pack so I could run the boat when he wasn't available."

I interrupted. "A six-pack? Like in beer?"

"No, it's not beer. It's a commercial boat captain's license. It allows you to legally take up to six paying passengers out on the water. You have to have one if you want to be a fishing guide or tour boat operator.

"Anyway, Captain Frank's health was failing and he was happy to let me handle the boat on the days he couldn't make it in.

"Nine months after I started working with him, he dropped dead at home. Heart attack.

"His wife listed the boat for sale with a broker and moved back up north. That left me with no job and no boat. That was three years ago.

"Even though I had my license, there weren't many captain jobs available. Most boat owners ran their own boat. They didn't want to pay someone else to do it, especially a girl.

"So I needed work. I looked around and found a part-time job at the kayak store in Nokomis. When they learned about my captain's license, they let me handle their kayak tours. It didn't pay much, but I learned what people wanted to see on the tours.

"I eventually bought some used kayaks and started doing tours on my own.

"I created a web page, uploaded some YouTube videos, and put flyers in all the tourist spots.

"Surprisingly, things worked out. The business took off and now I rarely have a day when I don't have a tour lined up."

I was impressed. Sarah had built her own business. A successful one at that.

"So, you have a boat captain's license, your own business, and your own fleet of boats. And yet you're still single?"

She made a face. "Did Molly tell you to say that? She's always trying to fix me up with someone. Probably with you too. But don't get your hopes up. After the last guy, I've sworn off men. I'm going to concentrate on my business and forget about relationships."

I decided to change the subject.

"So tell me the story of Mango Bob. How'd he get that name?"

Chapter 57

We were still sitting on the sand at Manasota Beach. Sarah was telling me about Mango Bob.

"When I first came to Englewood, I was looking for a place to rent. I couldn't afford much. Most places were way beyond my budget.

"A friend suggested I talk to Audrey Snyder. She was looking for a caretaker for the old boatyard. Someone to watch over the place in case things needed fixing. Broken windows, leaky pipes, rats. That kind of thing.

"The building had been empty for years and she'd had many offers to buy it, especially during the real estate boom. But she didn't want to sell.

"She told me her husband, Bob, bought the building when they first married. They planned to turn the back lot into a boat storage yard and call the place Bob's Boat Storage.

"But there was another Bob who had a boatyard in Englewood. Having two with the same name would be confusing. Since their boatyard was on Mango Street they named it Mango Bob's.

"Mrs. Snyder took a liking to me and agreed to rent the place to me for almost nothing as long as I agreed to be the caretaker. There was no way I could pass it up, so I moved in.

"The first night that I was there, I heard a yowling out in the boatyard. When I went to check, I saw this scrawny little kitten with no tail.

"He ran right up to the door and followed me in like he knew the place.

"He looked hungry so I fed him some tuna, gave him a

bowl of water and he settled right in.

"He was so tame I figured he belonged to someone in the neighborhood, so I posted signs. After three weeks, no one had claimed him.

"Mrs. Snyder came by one day and I showed her the kitty. She had a 'no pets' rule and I wanted her to know I was trying to find him a home.

She saw how cute and lovable the little kitty was and said, 'No way you're going to give up that cat. He's found you for a reason. He's yours. It won't hurt to have him around the boatyard. He'll keep the lizards and mice at bay.'

"So, with her blessings, I kept the cat.

"With his bobtail, I naturally called him Bob. And then Mango Bob because I found him on Mango Street in Mango Bob's old boatyard.

"He's been with me ever since. Except for this past summer when I let that low-life Eddie convince me that Mango Bob needed to go.

"Next time I'll know better. I'll keep Bob, dump the boyfriend."

She stood. "Let's go home. I want to see my Mango Bob."

Chapter 58

We were on the way back to the boatyard. Sarah was driving.

"I'm giving a kayak training session in the morning. You want to come?"

"Sure, sounds like fun. What time and what do I need to bring?"

"It's scheduled for nine at Indian Mound Park. Be ready to leave at eight.

"Wear a hat, sunglasses, sunscreen, short pants, and tennis shoes. Bring a towel because you're going to get wet. You have everything?"

"Yeah, all but the shorts. Will jeans be okay?"

"They'll do. But you'll need to get some Florida clothes if you plan to stay long."

We pulled into the boatyard driveway. Sarah handed me a key and said, "Keep this with you. You'll need it. It unlocks the gate."

After I got out and opened the gate, she pulled the truck in and parked. She got out, turned to me and said, "I hope you don't mind, but I'm not really set up to take Bob tonight. I don't have a litter box or kitty food.

"Maybe tomorrow, after we do the kayak training, we can get the things I need and move him over then.

"But I do want to see him tonight. Would you mind if I came over to your place? To see Bob?"

I smiled. "I wouldn't mind it a bit. Come on over. I'm sure he'd love to see you."

We went over to the RV. Before going in, I said, "He's been good about not trying to escape, but let's be careful."

I opened the door just far enough to make sure he wasn't on the other side waiting to get the jump on us. He wasn't. He was nowhere in sight.

"All clear, we can go in."

Sarah went in first and I followed, turning on the lights. She stopped at the couch and after looking around, called out for her kitty. "Bob? Are you in here? Bob?"

There was no response. She called out again. "Bob, where's my Bob? I know you're in here. Come see me."

Again, no response. We didn't hear his voice and he didn't come running.

I figured he was sleeping. I went to the back bedroom and, just as I suspected he was stretched out on the bed, his head on my pillow.

I hated to disturb him, but it was for a good cause. A reunion with Sarah.

I leaned over and gently touched his head. "Bob, there's someone here to see you."

He yawned, blinked his eyes, and said, "Murrph?"

I took it to mean he was wondering why I was waking him from his nap. He didn't like it when his sleep was interrupted.

Back in the front of the RV, Sarah called out his name. "Bob?"

His radar ears immediately tuned toward her voice. He remembered who she was. But he wasn't going to act too excited. He yawned and jumped down from the bed. He went into the bathroom and checked his food and water and then casually strolled to the front.

When Sarah saw him, her eyes lit up. "Bob. Is that you?

248

Did you miss me?"

He said, "Murrph."

She sat on the floor and he padded over to her. He rubbed his head against her leg and Sarah took it to mean he wanted to be petted. She began stroking his back and gently pulling his ears. He apparently liked or remembered her touch and started purring. Loudly.

She continued to pet him, giving him long strokes from his head to his stubby tail, all the while telling him how much she'd missed him. After a few minutes, he rolled over, letting her rub his belly.

She looked up at me. "Did you teach him that? He never used to let anyone rub him there. Now he does?"

I nodded. "Yeah, that's one of the many tricks I taught him. I've also taught him to cry before he poops. You'll love that one. And bark at squirrels. That's something else he can do now. And the best thing is I've taught him to sleep on top of me at night."

"You let him sleep with you? Most guys don't like a cat in bed with them."

I laughed. "I didn't really have a choice. He didn't ask if I wanted him on my bed. I just woke up and he was there."

She smiled. "You really do like him, don't you?"

I shrugged. "Yeah, I guess I do."

Chapter 59

Sarah was sitting on the floor petting Bob. He was enjoying the attention and showing it by purring and chirping.

She looked up at me. "Molly said you worked at the Conway plant for three years. What did you do before that?"

I didn't know whether she was really interested or was just making small talk. It would have been rude not to answer. "Before Conway, I worked as a computer security analyst for FMC."

"FMC? Never heard of them. What do they do?"

"They make weapons. Big ones. Tanks, missile launchers, those kinds of things."

"What were you doing there? Something with computers?"

"Yeah, they hired me to try to hack into their computer networks. They wanted me to find security holes and to track down anyone who tried to get into the system illegally."

"Sounds interesting. So you were a paid hacker?"

"Yeah, something like that. But it was all, well mostly, legal."

"Before that, you were in the service, right?"

"Yeah. Six years. Spent most of it in Afghanistan."

"Did you get shot at?"

"Every day. But the heat was the real killer. Bad on our weapons, our communications gear, our people.

"I was glad to get out alive. Six years working for Uncle Sam was enough for me."

251

She smiled. "So I'm guessing you know how to swim?"

"Yeah, I can swim. Learned when I was a kid. Spent my summers on the lake. Even worked as a lifeguard at a summer camp for two years."

"That's good to know. It'll mean that when we do the kayak training tomorrow, at least one person other than me can swim. That'll be you.

"By any chance do you know CPR?"

I laughed. "Why do you ask? You need it right now?"

"No, I'm serious. Do you know CPR?"

"Yeah, I know how to do CPR. And battlefield first aid. I've had lots of experience doing both."

She looked impressed. "I've never had to perform CPR in an emergency situation. But I did have to take a CPR course as part of my captain's training. It'll be good that we both know how to do it."

I didn't want to think about CPR or the times I had to try it on the battlefield. The memories were painful. I changed the subject.

"So, tell me about working as a boat captain. Is it profitable?"

She looked up from Bob. "Profitable? No, not really. We could only work when the weather was right and when we had at least three customers.

"In a good week, we'd bring in a few thousand.

"Out of that we'd have to pay for fuel, dock fees and insurance.

"After expenses, the captain would be lucky to end up with a thousand profit for the week. That money didn't last long if the boat had mechanical problems or needed repairs. It almost always did.

"So no, you don't get rich being a boat captain. In fact, it's a good way to go broke. But if I had a big enough boat, I'd still be out there every day. It's something that gets in your blood."

She paused, obviously thinking about her life at sea.

I took the opportunity to ask another question. "So, if you could afford a boat, what kind would you get, and what would you do with it?"

She smiled. "I've thought about that a lot.

"If I won the lottery, I'd get a thirty-six-foot catamaran and offer nature and kayak tours out on the barrier islands. Maybe even take longer tours down into the keys or overnights into the Thousand Islands.

"The catamaran's shallow draft would let me go places other boats couldn't get to. It'd have enough cabin space for six people double-bunking.

"If it were a motor-sailer, I could keep the fuel costs low and offer the kind of eco-friendly tours people want these days. And Bob could go along. I think he'd like it.

"But unless I win the lottery, it won't happen."

"Why is that?"

"Because even a very used thirty-six-foot cat will cost seventy-five grand. At the rate I'm going, I'll never have that much money."

I nodded. "Yeah, I know what you mean. Still, it's nice to have a dream."

She stood. "Time for me to go. I've had a long day and have to get up early in the morning. If you're going to go out on the water with me, you need to be ready to help me load the boats around eight."

Bob swatted at her ankle playfully and she bent over to

talk to him. "Bob, you spend the night here tonight. Tomorrow we'll move you back home. Is that okay?"

He looked up and said, "Murrph?"

She gave him a reassuring pet then looked at me. "You'll be okay with him here one more night, right?"

"Yeah, no problem. I think he likes it here."

She shook her head. "Don't get too attached. Tomorrow he's moving in with me. See you in the morning."

She went to the door and let herself out.

Bob watched her leave, then said, "Murrph."

I nodded and said, "I know what you mean."

Chapter 60

Thirty minutes after Sarah left, my phone chimed with a call from Molly.

I answered.

Before I could say anything, she asked, "So how was your date with Sarah?"

"Molly, it wasn't a date. Just dinner and talk."

"Walker, come on. Give me something to work with. What do you think about her?"

"Molly, she seems like a fine person. Has an interesting life. No bad habits I've discovered so far."

"So are you going to ask her out again?"

"Molly, I'm living in her back yard. I guess we'll be seeing a lot of each other. Maybe even eating a meal or two together."

"Woohoo! I knew you two would hit it off. You're perfect for each other."

"Molly, I've got to go. It's been a long day. I'll talk to you later."

I ended the call.

It was getting late. Time to close the shades and get ready for bed.

Bob agreed. He was already on my pillow when I got there.

I set the alarm for six thirty. I wanted to get up early, take a walk. Get a feel for the neighborhood. Then be ready for Sarah at eight.

Chapter 61

My phone chimed me awake telling me it was time to get up.

Bob was still asleep. He wasn't an early riser and was on the bed with one paw over my foot. As I moved he said, "Murrph." Then he flexed his claws, showing me who was boss.

"Yeah Bob, I know you're there. I'm getting up anyway."

He said, "Murrph." Then he moved his paw off my foot and went back to sleep.

I got up and took care of my morning business. Ran a hand through my hair, pulled on a sweatshirt, a pair of jeans, and running shoes. I grabbed my keys and wallet and headed out.

It wasn't quite daylight yet. The eastern sky was showing the promise of morning, but stars were still visible in the west.

I slipped out the gate, locking it behind me, being as quiet as possible. I didn't want to wake Sarah.

Remembering the layout of the area from Google Maps, I planned to walk to the end of Dearborn where it met Lemon Bay then follow Old Englewood Road to Lemon Bay Park, then back to Dearborn.

It'd be about three miles and give me a chance to check out the neighborhood and see the waters of the bay.

As I headed down Dearborn, I took note of the different shops. An old five and dime. A soda fountain. A hardware store. A barbershop. A few antique stores. Three art galleries.

Not a single fast-food joint. No cookie-cutter mall stores. Just a slice of what main street America looked like forty years ago.

Being so early in the morning, all the shops were closed except one. The Corner Market at the intersection of Dearborn and Old Englewood Road.

Even at this early hour, it seemed to be doing a brisk business. Trucks pulling fishing boats filled the parking lot. As soon as one pulled out, another pulled in.

As I got closer, I could see why.

In addition to the standard convenience store fare, the Dearborn Corner Market had aerator tanks outside filled with the kind of fresh bait fishermen wanted. Live shrimp.

With the boat launch just three blocks away, it was easy to see why fishermen stopped there. They could get hot coffee, cold beer, and fresh bait. A fisherman's dream.

I continued my walk to Lemon Bay Park, passing through neighborhoods of small, well-kept homes. Many had a boat parked in the driveway or off to the side of the house. With Lemon Bay and the Gulf of Mexico so close, it made sense.

People living in these neighborhoods could launch their boats and Jet Skis from any of the nearby ramps and be on the water in minutes.

At Lemon Bay Park, I took a few minutes to check out the information kiosk and the map of the nearby trails and waterways. A sign warned that gators, Florida panthers and bobcats were known to live nearby. I didn't see any on my walk through the park but was glad to know that wildlife thrived in the area.

Leaving the park, I headed back toward Dearborn and stopped at the Corner Market.

Inside, I picked out a mesh ball cap, a pair of cheap sunglasses, a tube of SPF 50 sunscreen, and an "Englewood, Florida" T-shirt.

The young lady at the checkout said, "Looks like you're planning a day on the water. You need any bait to go with that?"

"No, no bait today. Just doing some kayaking."

She smiled as she rang me up. "It'll be a good day for it. The water's supposed to be calm through this afternoon.

"You need anything else? Maybe a lottery ticket?"

I wasn't much of a gambler and, in fact, had never bought a lottery ticket in my life. But maybe it was my lucky day.

"Yeah, a lottery ticket sounds good. I'll take one."

The clerk smiled and said, "Which one do you want?"

I shrugged. "I don't know. I'm new to this. What do you suggest?"

"Get all three. Florida Lottery. Power Ball. And Mega Millions. That'll increase your chances of winning."

"Okay, I'll take one of each."

"Total for all this along with the lottery tickets will be thirty-seven dollars and ninety-five cents."

I paid with two twenties.

Handing me the change, the cashier said, "Good luck with the lottery. And welcome to Florida."

I nodded. "Thanks."

Back outside, I checked the shrimp in the fish tanks. They looked pretty much like what we had eaten the night before. But they were alive and still had their heads with their beady black eyes.

It was almost seven-thirty. The sun was up, the sky was a deep blue. The temperature in the mid-fifties and starting to climb. From the market to my motorhome was an easy five-minute walk.

If I timed it right, I would be able to get back, shower, shave, eat breakfast, and still have a few minutes before meeting Sarah for the Kayak training.

Back at the boatyard, the lights in her apartment weren't yet on. This meant I had plenty of time to get ready.

As I unlocked the door to the motorhome, Bob came running from the back and said, "Murrph."

I gave him a rub, which seemed to satisfy him. He turned and walked back toward the bathroom saying, "MURRPH." This time much louder.

Apparently he wanted me to follow.

When I caught up with him, he was rubbing against the bathroom door, still talking to me. "MURRRPHH!"

His food bowl was empty. His litter box full.

I poured him some food. Then scooped up little dumplings out of his litter box. I put them in a plastic bag from Walmart, tied off the top, and took it to the front door. I'd deal with it later.

Bob checked his freshly cleaned box and said, "Murrph." He was pleased. Then he climbed back into bed. He'd successfully gotten me to do for him. Now he needed his rest.

For me, it was time for a quick shower, which meant moving his litter box out of the shower stall and into the hallway. After doing that, I undressed, turned on the shower, and got in.

There was no hot water. I had forgotten to turn the water heater on. Since I was already wet, a quick cold shower would have to do.

I followed it with a cold shave then put on jeans, tennis shoes, and my new T-shirt with a sweatshirt over it.

Before leaving the bathroom, I remembered to move Bob's

litter box back into the shower stall. He'd be upset if I forgot.

For breakfast, I had cold cereal. White grape juice poured over Raisin Bran. It sounds weird but tastes pretty good.

Just as I was finishing up, I heard Sarah at the door. "Walker. Time to get up. We've got work to do."

"I'm up. Just enjoying a little breakfast with Bob. Have you eaten yet?"

"Yep, eggs and juice. About an hour ago."

"Okay. I'll be right there."

When I went outside, she was busy wiping the morning dew off the kayaks. Seeing me, she said, "Morning, sleepyhead. You ready to go out on the water?"

"I am. Been up for three hours. Checked out Dearborn Street and Lemon Bay early this morning."

"Good to hear that you've got all that energy. It'll come in handy later on.

"So here's the deal. Before we go out to meet clients, we have to get everything ready. We start by getting the boats on the trailer. Then we check that we have paddles and life jackets for each one.

"After that, we make sure we have a first aid kit, extra hats, sunscreen, dry towels, and a twelve-pack of bottled water. Everything goes into the truck.

"Once the truck is loaded, we hook up the trailer and head out. We're scheduled to meet our group at Indian Mound Park at nine thirty. We want to get there twenty minutes early to reserve our spot."

She was loading the truck and pointing things out as she was talking. When we'd gotten everything in, she said, "Okay, the truck's loaded. Time to get the trailer hitched up. See if you can do it by yourself."

It didn't look too difficult. The trailer was pretty light, and all I needed to do was to pull it close to the truck, drop the hitch on the ball, snap the lock, and connect the safety chains.

When I had finished, she inspected my work. "Good job. Looks like you've done this before."

"Many times." I didn't tell her that during my tours in Afghanistan we hitched far heavier trailers carrying weapons and gear every day.

She looked at how I was dressed. "You wearing jeans? We're going to be in the water. They're going to get wet and heavy with the salt."

"Yeah, I know. But jeans are all I have. I haven't had time to get shorts."

"Okay, jeans will have to do. But if you buy me lunch, I'll take you clothes shopping later on today."

I wasn't sure I wanted her, or any woman to take me clothes shopping. Lunch I could handle. If that meant I had to go shopping with her after, I would.

I tried my best to sound like I was looking forward to it. "That sounds like fun. Anything else I need this morning?"

"Yeah, sunscreen, hat, and sunglasses."

"I've got them in the coach. I'll go get them."

I went back to the motorhome checked on Bob and made sure he had plenty of water. The perfect weather meant I could leave the windows open. He'd like that.

On my way out, I grabbed the sunscreen, my new ball cap, sunglasses and keys. I didn't think I'd need my cell phone. I left it in the charger.

As always, I locked the door behind me.

Sarah was waiting. "Nice looking hat. Where'd you get it?"

"At the Dearborn Corner Market. I got something there for you too."

I pulled out the three lottery tickets from my wallet and handed them to her.

"Lottery tickets? You bought me lottery tickets?"

"Yeah, last night you said you needed to win the lottery to get the boat you wanted. So here you go."

She took them. "Thanks. Maybe today is my lucky day."

Chapter 62

After I opened the gate Sarah drove the truck pulling the trailer out into the street. I locked the gate and got in with her.

"The gate locked?"

"Yep. Double-checked it."

"Good. We always lock it when we leave.

"So here's the deal. Today, we've got a class at Indian Mound Park on Lemon Bay. It's about five minutes from here.

"There are four women in the class and they want to learn the basics of kayaking.

"I'll be doing the training. You'll be my assistant. Your job is to unload the boats and do whatever else I tell you.

"If anyone in the class asks you questions, you refer them to me. That way they'll understand I'm the lead and you're the assistant.

"These are older ladies, and if you want to flirt with them, that's fine. But nothing more than innocent flirting, okay?"

"Yeah, I got it. You're the leader. I'm the assistant. Easy on the flirting."

When we got to Indian Mound Park, we drove past the boat launch to a parking area near a small sandy beach.

As I started to get out, Sarah stopped me. "Hang on. No need to start unloading until the clients get here."

"Okay. Just tell me when."

She pointed over her shoulder. "There's a restroom over there. If you need to go, now's a good time. Before we get out on the water."

I smiled. "Maybe I'll check it out. Be right back."

The restrooms were sparse but had the necessary facilities. There was an information kiosk nearby showing the history of the park.

According to it, the place was the site of several prehistoric shell middens, dating back more than three thousand years. The original mounds were built by native tribes using discarded oyster shells, which were abundant in the bay. The middens provided high ground during tidal flooding and shelter during tropical storms.

The kiosk had a map and more history; I didn't have time to read it all. I needed to get back to Sarah.

When I got to the truck, she was talking with two older women. Seeing me coming, she turned and said, "Ladies, this is Walker. He's helping us out today. If you have any questions about kayaking, ask me. If you need something hauled or lifted, he's your guy."

The two ladies smiled and introduced themselves.

Sarah turned to me. "Time to unload the boats. Get them off the trailer and line them up on the beach over there. Leave about three feet between each one.

"If you need any help lifting them, let me know."

The boats were light and she knew I wouldn't need her help. But at least she offered.

I went to the trailer and started on the boats. Each weighed about forty pounds. Easy to handle.

The distance from the trailer to the sandy beach was about thirty feet. I carried each boat over and lined them up as instructed by Sarah. As I was putting the last one on the sand, she came over and said, "Good job. Now put a life jacket and paddle in each one."

While I was doing this, two more women arrived. Both looked to be in their mid-fifties.

Sarah introduced me again. "Ladies, this is Walker. He's our gopher today. If you need anything involving muscle, ask him.

"If you have questions about kayaking or safety, ask me.

"We're going to start our training in about ten minutes. We'll do thirty minutes on shore then about an hour in the water.

"During the water sessions, you're going to get your feet and legs wet. Wear shoes that you don't mind getting soaked in salt water.

"There's a bathroom in the pavilion over there. If you need to use it, now is a good time. If you haven't applied sunscreen, do it now. If you didn't bring any, I've got some in the truck.

"Any questions?"

One of the ladies raised her hand. "Are there sharks or alligators in the water?"

Sarah smiled. "No, you don't have to worry about them. It's been a long time since anyone has seen either out here."

Another lady raised her hand. "Should I wear my swimsuit?"

Sarah smiled again. "The water's a little cool for swimming, but the sun will warm us up later on. If you brought your swimsuit, feel free to wear it."

The lady who asked the first question raised her hand again. "Why is Walker wearing jeans? Isn't he going to get in the water?"

Sarah looked at me and laughed. "He's wearing jeans because he just got here from up north yesterday and didn't have sense enough to bring shorts with him. But don't worry. I'm taking him shopping later today to get him the kind of clothes he needs. I'm sure he'll enjoy the experience."

All of the women laughed. I didn't understand why but would soon find out.

Chapter 63

Sarah continued, "Ladies, we'll be starting in ten minutes. If you need to change or use the restrooms, do it now. If you have valuables in your car, put them in the trunk lock the doors."

The women took off toward their cars and then the pavilion.

Kaye, the woman who had asked about wearing a bathing suit, was the first one back. She had on a skimpy hot-pink two-piece suit, which revealed a surprisingly nice body for a woman in her late forties.

The other women returned wearing shorts and T-shirts.

Sarah stood in front of them and said, "Let's get started."

For the first ten minutes, she explained the basics of kayaking. Then she showed the features of each boat.

She explained that Florida law required kayakers to have a life jacket, either on or within reach in the boat, and a sound-producing device like a whistle, also in easy reach.

She then demonstrated how to put on and adjust the life jackets found in each boat. She also showed how to use the whistle, which was attached by a cord to each jacket.

"Now that we've covered the basics, choose the boat you want. They're all the same except the colors."

We'd brought six boats. Enough for everyone in the class, plus one for Sarah and one for me. The women took their time examining each of the kayaks, trying to find just the right one.

Sarah had been through this before and gave them time to make their selections. When everyone had chosen one, she said, "Okay, now that you've got your boat, put on your life jacket. I'll come around and check to make sure it's on correctly."

With their life jackets securely on, Sarah continued her training for another twenty minutes. She stood in the water and showed her students how to safely get in and out of a kayak, how to keep from rolling over, and how to get back in should they fall out in deep water.

After the safety lessons, she showed how to paddle efficiently, how to keep dry when paddling, and how to hold the paddle to keep from getting blisters.

Finally she said, "Okay ladies, time for you to get in your boats and paddle out to me. Take your time. Do it just like I showed you. Walker will be on shore to help you if you run into problems."

One by one, the women got into their boats and, with a little effort, were able to launch into the water and paddle out to Sarah.

I got into the remaining boat and joined the class on the water.

Sarah said, "Okay, we're going to paddle single file over to the mangroves and stop there. I'll lead the way and Walker will bring up the rear.

"If you have any problems, blow your whistle and I'll come back to assist you.

"Any questions?"

No one spoke up.

"Okay, let's head out. Follow me, and try to paddle the way I showed you.

She turned and slowly paddled, staying close to the shore and avoiding the center of the bay where boat traffic was starting to pick up.

Three of her four students followed her closely. But one, the lady in the hot pink swimsuit, lagged behind.

I quickly caught up with her. "We need to stay close to the group. Stay up with Sarah."

"Walker. That's what Sarah said your name was, right? I'm Kaye."

"Glad to meet you, Kaye. Let's catch up with the rest of the group."

"What's your hurry? You can give me private lessons back here."

Kaye had stopped paddling.

"No, we need to stay with the group. Let's catch up."

Kaye dropped her paddle in the water. "Oops! Dropped my paddle. I need your help."

I could see this was going to be a problem.

I paddled over, picked up her paddle, and handed it to her. She grabbed it and pulled me in close.

As my boat bounced off of hers, she said, "Come on, Walker, what are you afraid of?"

As I turned to answer, I heard a whistle followed by Sarah calling out, "Walker, I need you up here."

I pushed off Kaye's boat and began paddling toward Sarah at the front of the group. Kaye followed and coasted to a stop near the other women.

As I got close to Sarah's boat, she said, "A little closer, please."

I paddled until our boats touched, side by side.

We were in front of the class when Sarah said, "Ladies, we're going to see if Walker was paying attention when I showed you how to get back into a kayak while in deep water."

She grabbed the side of my kayak, lifted it up, and dumped me into the water.

"Okay, show us what you learned."

I was in the water, hanging on to my boat. Wet from head to toe. My jeans dragging me down.

Trying not to embarrass myself, I remembered what Sarah had shown us earlier.

First step, roll the kayak over so the cockpit was right side up. That was easy.

Then reach across to the opposite side with one hand and grip the near side with the other.

With the boat upright and steady, I pulled with both hands and slid on my belly. When my hips were across the open cockpit, I rolled over, dropping my butt into the seat.

Then I lifted my left leg, heavy with the wet denim, and dropped it into the cockpit. I did the same with my right and was finally back in.

The women in the group applauded.

Sarah smiled. "Not bad. But let me ask you a question.

"Where's your paddle?"

I looked around and didn't see it.

Sarah pointed out into the bay, about forty feet from my boat.

"It's over there. The current's picked it up. You'd be in trouble if I weren't here to retrieve it for you.

She spoke to the class. "There's an important lesson here; always keep control of your paddle. If you fall out of your boat, be sure to grab your paddle right away and secure it to the boat before you try to get back in."

"Any questions?"

Kaye, the swimsuit gal, raised her hand. "What about Walker? He's over there soaking wet. Without a paddle. You want me to go help him?"

Sarah shook her head. "Don't worry about him. I'll get his paddle; then we're going to head to shore where we'll practice getting out of the boats without tipping over."

She power-stroked out to my paddle, secured it under the bungee cords on her kayak and brought it back to me.

As she got close, she whispered, "Seems like you have a new special friend. You and her have plans for later on?"

She handed me the paddle. "See if you can keep up with the rest of us."

She turned toward her class. "Any other questions?"

One of the women raised her hand. "When can we go on a longer tour? I want to see dolphins."

"Good question. We do longer four-hour tours most days of the week. During these, we paddle out to Stump Pass where we stop and have a snack. Then we'll paddle out into the gulf where we usually see dolphins.

"If you visit our website, you can see photos and sign up for these longer tours."

She pointed to the beach. "Okay, it's time for us to head to shore. Back to where we launched the boats."

Sarah led the way, with the class following. I brought up the rear.

On shore, she demonstrated how to get out of a kayak without tipping over. She then helped each member of the class get out of their boat.

She didn't bother helping me.

When we were all back on dry land, she spoke to the group. "I hope you enjoyed your tour this morning. Are there any questions I didn't answer?"

No one had questions, but the women agreed they'd had a great time. They were happy with what they had learned and confident they could handle a kayak.

Two of the ladies said they'd be signing up for a trip later on in the week.

Swimsuit Kaye asked Sarah if I would be going on the longer trips.

She smiled and said, "It depends. Walker hasn't decided how long he's going to be in Florida. After this morning's baptism, he might not want to go back out in a kayak. At least with me."

The women laughed.

As they began packing and returning to their cars, one of the ladies came up to me and said, "You and Sarah are such a cute couple!"

I laughed. "Sarah and me? A couple? No way, we just met yesterday."

"Really? Well, you've got chemistry. Probably some interesting times ahead for both of you. Take care."

She walked away just as Sarah called my name. "Walker, you're supposed to be helping me. You need to get these boats on the trailer."

I walked to the boats, thinking about what the woman had said about interesting times ahead. Maybe she was right.

Chapter 64

"Was the water cold?"

We were back in the truck, Sarah was driving.

I was soaking wet. Trying my manly best not to shiver. "If you really want to know, let's go back. I'll dump you in the water and you can tell me whether it is cold or not."

She laughed. "Don't be that way. I was just trying to save you from the gal in the swimsuit."

"Yeah right, like I needed saving."

When we reached the boatyard, I got out without saying anything and unlocked the gate. Sarah pulled into the yard and backed the trailer close to the wash-down station.

After spraying the boats, we each grabbed a sponge and went to work. We'd cleaned half them when Sarah came over and said, "Walker, you did good out there. You're a natural."

She was trying to make nice. But I wasn't going to let her off the hook so easily. I grabbed the water hose, pointed it at her, and said, "I think I missed a spot."

I was tempted to pull the trigger but didn't. We both didn't need to be wet. I dropped the hose and picked up my sponge.

She came over, put her hand on my shoulder and said, "You weren't really thinking about spraying me, were you?"

I smiled.

She took my sponge. "I'll do the rest. You go in and change into dry clothes. Meet me back out here in twenty minutes. We'll go get lunch.

"Be sure to bring your credit card. We're going to get you

the right kind of clothes for Florida."

Back inside the motorhome, I checked on Bob. He was still sleeping, something he was good at.

Remembering the cold shower from that morning, I switched on the water heater. While waiting for it to heat up, I stripped out of my clothes and checked my closet.

Five days on the road and I was running out of anything clean to wear. I'd need to find a laundromat soon.

I grabbed a dry pair of jeans and a shirt I'd only worn once. They'd have to do.

The hot shower felt good. I was still drying off when Sarah banged on the door.

"Come on, Walker. You take longer than a girl!"

I smiled and said, "I can come out naked if you want. But if you give me a minute, I'll be dressed and ready."

From outside, I heard her say, "Don't come out here naked. No one wants to see that. Just hurry."

I pulled on my jeans and shirt, ran a hand through my hair, and grabbed my wallet and keys. No need for the cell phone; I left it in the charger. On the way out, I locked the door behind me.

Outside, Sarah was hanging wet life jackets onto the top rail of the kayak trailer.

She looked up. "Got your wallet?"

"Yep."

"Good. You still mad at me for dunking you? You going to pout all day?"

"I'm not pouting. I'm planning my revenge."

"Oh, I'm in trouble now. Walker is out to get me."

She pointed to the truck. "You can have your revenge

later. But right now, let's go get you some Florida clothes. That way it won't be so bad next time you get dunked."

I smiled. "Don't be so sure it'll be me who gets dunked next time."

Chapter 65

"Okay, Walker. Enough of this. We're going shopping and after that, you're buying me lunch."

She started the truck and drove out the gate without me. She stopped on the street and waited while I closed and locked the gate.

As soon as I got in the truck, we were off. East on Dearborn then right on 776. Through three stoplights. Past McDonald's at Beach Road.

I was trying to identify buildings and streets I could use as waypoints so if I drove I wouldn't get lost. But really, with the Gulf of Mexico on one side and 776 on the other, finding my way around Englewood would be pretty easy.

After about eight minutes Sarah pulled into the Merchants Crossing Shopping Center and parked in front of a Bealls department store.

She said, "We're here," and got out of the truck. She headed toward the store. I followed.

Inside, she walked to the men's department, looked around, and went to a display of Columbia fishing shirts.

"You'll need at least four of these. They'll keep you cool. They dry quickly and have plenty of pockets for gear.

"You probably wear a large. Hold out your arms."

She picked out four shirts, yellow, orange, green, and light blue, and piled them in my outstretched arms.

She pointed to a display stacked with men's canvas shorts. "You look like a large, but you'll want to try them on just in case." She handed me a pair and pointed to her right. "Men's dressing room is over there."

I took the shorts into the dressing room and tried them on. Just as I was zipping up the fly, Sarah knocked and said, "Come out; let me see how they fit."

"They fit fine. I'll be out in a minute."

I changed back into my jeans and went out carrying the shorts.

She looked amused. "Too embarrassed to show your lily-white legs? No problem, we'll have you tanned up in no time.

"If those fit, get four pair."

I went back to the display and added three to the one I was carrying. With shirts and shorts, I figured we were done. But I was wrong. Sarah was still in shopping mode.

"You need T-shirts. Things you can wear while working around the boatyard. The Columbia PFG tees are a good choice."

I followed her to a table piled high with brightly colored shirts. She picked out five and added them to the stack of clothes I was carrying.

"Last thing we need to get you are ankle socks. Let's get ten pair."

She grabbed a package of ten and added them to the pile.

"That should do it. Anything else you can think of?"

I shook my head. "I'm carrying more clothes than I've ever bought at one time in my life. Are you sure I need all this?"

"Yes, you need them. You'll soon be thanking me. Now, let's check out."

We walked to the nearest cashier. The total bill was $237.50. I paid with a credit card.

As we walked back out to the truck, Sarah asked, "So, what's for lunch?"

I pointed to the Subway sandwich shop across the street. "That works for me. How about you?"

"Oh goody! I'm out with a big spender." Then, "Just kidding, Subway sounds good."

We went in and ordered our sandwiches and drinks. The girl behind the counter got them ready quickly and I paid.

We picked out a table and started in on our lunch.

After a few bites, Sarah asked, "So what do you think so far?"

"About what?"

"Englewood. Florida. Kayaking. Me."

I pretended to chew before I answered. Then I swallowed and said, "I've only been here a day. So far, it's been fun. Great weather. Nice people."

She nodded. "Think you'll stick around for a while?"

I couldn't think of a reason not to. I had a free place to camp close to the water, a town I felt comfortable in, and Sarah to show me around.

"Yeah, I pretty much have to now that you made me buy all those clothes."

She poked me with her straw. "I did you a favor. Having the right clothes when working on the water will make a big difference. You'll see.

"Speaking of which, I've got a kayak tour scheduled tomorrow afternoon. Three of the ladies from this morning signed up, along with three others who signed up earlier.

"You want to go out with us? Be my assistant again?"

I took a bite of my sandwich and chewed without answering.

"I promise not to turn your boat over."

I smiled. "I'll think about it."

As we finished our meal, she said, "On the way back I need to stop at PetSmart. Gotta get some stuff for Bob so I can move him over to my place."

I nodded. "There's no need to be in a rush to move him. He can stay with me a little longer. He's no trouble."

"Walker, you've had him long enough. This afternoon he's moving back in with me."

PetSmart was across the street from Subway. We drove over and Sarah went in. I followed.

She picked out a large litter box, a twenty-pound bucket of litter, and a five-pound bag of Maxicat roasted chicken kibble, which apparently was Bob's favorite.

After paying for the supplies, we left the store, got in the truck, and headed back to the boatyard.

Traffic was light. It took just a few minutes to get there.

As we pulled up to the yard, Sarah said, "The gate's open. Didn't we lock it when we left?"

"Yeah, I locked it. Anyone else have a key?"

"No, just you and me."

She pulled into the lot.

The Love Bus was gone. With Bob inside.

Chapter 66

Sarah looked at me. "Where's your RV?"

"I have no idea. It was here when we left. I locked the door. I have the keys in my pocket. Someone must have taken it. With Bob inside."

She shook her head. "Call nine one one."

I reached for my phone, then remembered I'd left it on the charger inside the Love Bus.

"Can't. No phone. It's in the motorhome."

She pulled out hers. "I'll call. But you'll have to do the talking."

After dialing 911, she handed me the phone.

"Nine one one. What is your emergency?"

"My motorhome was just stolen."

Calmly, the operator asked, "Has anyone been hurt?"

"No, but my motorhome is gone, it's been stolen. Everything I own is inside. With Bob."

"Bob? A child?"

"No, not a child. He's my cat. He was sleeping in the back."

The operator said, "Hold please."

She came back a few moments later. "Sir, a stolen vehicle isn't considered an emergency. I can contact the sheriff's office and ask them to call you for a follow-up. Would you like me to do that?"

"Yes. Please."

I heard a few clicks, then, "Okay, I've forwarded the

information to the sheriff. They will call you back in a few.

"Is there any other emergency you wish to report?"

"No." I hung up and gave Sarah her phone.

"They said a stolen vehicle isn't an emergency. They're going to alert the sheriff. Someone is supposed to follow up with us later."

Sarah was visibly upset. "So what do we do? I've got to get Bob back."

I didn't know the answer but said, "We've been gone for less than an hour, they couldn't have gotten far.

"The RV was almost out of gas. They'll have to stop soon. Where's the nearest station big enough for an RV?"

Sarah thought for a moment, then said, "Pretty much every station in Florida can handle an RV. They could be at any of them."

Time was of the essence. We needed to figure out where the RV was, what direction it was going. I reached into my pocket planning to pull out my phone to look at Google maps. But remembered I'd left the phone in the RV.

Then it came to me. "My phone has a locator app on it. If I text a secret word to it, it will text me back the GPS location. Let me see your phone."

She handed it to me and I quickly texted the secret word to my phone.

Two minutes later, her phone chimed. A text message had arrived.

It showed the location of my phone, the speed and direction of travel, and included a link to a Google map showing a satellite view.

I clicked the link and it showed, "Walmart Super Center, Osprey."

I looked at Sarah. "How far is that?"

"It's on the north side of Venice, about thirty minutes away. Why?"

"That's where the motorhome is right now. Maybe we can get to it before they take off again. Do you know anyone you can call who might be able to get there quicker?"

She shook her head. "No, everyone I know lives here in Englewood."

I pulled out my wallet and looked for the card given to me by Jack, my RV friend. He'd said he and Jean would be staying in Venice.

Using Sarah's phone, I called his number. He answered on the second ring.

"Jack, this is Walker. My motorhome was stolen about an hour ago. Right now it's in the Walmart parking lot in Osprey. I'm heading that way to try to get it back.

"It'll take me thirty minutes to get there. I'm afraid it will be long gone by then.

"Is there any way you can get there quicker?"

"Yeah, I'm six minutes away, getting in the car right now."

"Good. When you get there, don't confront the guy. Just block him in."

"Walker, have you called the police?"

"Yeah, and they said it was a low-priority crime, not an emergency. Bob's in the motorhome. Along with everything I own. I don't want this guy to get away."

"Walker, don't worry, we'll get him. I'll call you back when I get there."

He ended the call.

Chapter 67

Sarah was driving as fast as traffic would allow. We got out of Englewood quickly, but traffic through Venice slowed to a crawl.

"Who was that?"

"Jack Daniels, a retired cop I met on my way down here.

"He and his wife are in Venice. He's going to try to get to Walmart and block the motorhome in so it can't go anywhere."

Gripping the wheel tightly, she asked, "What are you going to do when we get there? What if the guy is armed?"

"If he's armed, we'll call the police. I'm not worried about that. If we block him in, he won't be going anywhere. Even if he's armed he won't do anything stupid. Too many witnesses in the Walmart lot."

Sarah concentrated on getting through traffic, trying to dodge the snowbirds who seemed to block her at every turn.

She slammed her hand on the steering wheel. "Damn this traffic! We're not going to get there in time!"

Her phone chimed. It was Jack.

"Walker, I'm in the Walmart lot. Your rig is still here. No one's in it. I parked in front of it. It can't leave."

"Great! We're about six minutes away. Call me if anything happens." I hung up.

"Sarah, the motorhome is still there. No one inside it."

She was visibly relieved. "Maybe Bob's still in it. I hope he's okay."

Five miles past the Nokomis Beach turn-off, we saw the

Walmart sign in the distance. Sarah got into the right lane and when we finally got to the entrance, she pulled into Walmart.

The parking lot was big, filled with lots of cars. But it was easy to spot the motorhome. It was taller than all the other cars and stood out where it was parked in the far corner of the lot.

As we got closer, we could see a black Mercury Marauder parked in front of it. Jack was in his Florida car which looked like an undercover police cruiser. Maybe a retirement gift from Boston PD.

We parked behind the motorhome, boxing it in.

I got out and walked over to Jack. "Anything going on inside?"

"Not yet. Looks like nobody's home."

I patted my pocket. "I've got the keys; we could just take it back."

He shook his head. "Not a good idea. Better to find out who took it and why. Else they might come back and try to get it again."

A man carrying a Walmart bag in one hand, a tissue wiping his eyes with the other approached us.

Since there were no other vehicles parked nearby, we figured he was our guy. We stepped in front of him, blocking his path. He looked surprised.

I turned to Sarah. "Call the police. Tell them there's a disturbance in the Walmart parking lot. Tell them someone is going to get hurt."

The man looked confused. "What's this about?"

I pointed to the motorhome. "That's mine. It was stolen a few minutes ago. We're here to get it back."

The man held up both hands. "Hey, no need for violence. I'm just doing my job."

I looked at Jack then back at the man. "Your job? You stole my motorhome. That's not a job. That's a felony."

He shook his head. "You're wrong, I didn't steal it. I took it legally. I have a repossession order from the lien holder."

Chapter 68

"That can't be right. I own this vehicle free and clear. It's registered in my name. No liens."

The man shook his head. "That's not what I was told. I got a repo order. The paperwork's inside."

He reached for the door. I blocked his way.

"You're not going in. This is mine. There's no loan on it. Nothing to repossess."

The repo man stepped back. "Look, I've driven twelve hundred miles trying to get this RV and I'm not leaving without it. The client has already paid me. He sent me the keys and a link to the GPS tracker."

Jack interrupted him. "A legal repo requires you to have a copy of the title and the lien showing a delinquency. Let's see them."

The repo guy said nothing.

Jack repeated the request. "Let's see the paperwork. You do have it, don't you?"

The repo guy shook his head. "The client said he'd send it along with the keys and the payment.

"He paid in cash and sent the keys but no papers. I called but haven't been able to reach him.

"Since he paid me five thousand up front, I figured he'd be good for it."

I looked at the repo guy. "Here's the problem. I'm the legal owner of this motorhome. I have the registration and bill of sale in the glove box.

"So who's the client that's paying you?"

The repo guy pulled a note out of his shirt pocket and read the name. "Tucker. Harvey Tucker."

I looked at him, shaking my head. "Harvey Tucker never owned this RV. He rented it for a few days from the company that owned it. He probably made a copy of the keys then.

"The company sold it to me legally. Tucker has no claim against it.

"He tricked you into stealing it. You picked it up without the proper paperwork. That means you committed felony theft.

"There's one more thing you'll want to know. Tucker's dead. You won't be getting any more money from him."

A police car pulled up. The officer inside rolled down his window. "This the disturbance call?"

I nodded. "Yeah, it is. This guy stole that motorhome. It belongs to me. We're here to get it back."

The cop got out of his car and interviewed each of us individually. When he spoke to me, I showed him the registration and bill of sale. He called it in, along with the tag number.

After twenty minutes of interviews, he came over and said. "Your story checks out. The repo guy had no legal right to take your vehicle."

He continued, "It looks like he made an honest mistake. Relied on faulty information. But if you want to press charges, you can."

I thought about it for a moment. "Let me speak to him. See if I can clear this up."

I went over to the repo guy. "The officer says I can press felony theft charges against you. I haven't decided whether I will or not. If you answer some questions, it'll help me make up my mind.

"When Harvey Tucker called you, what'd he tell you to do with the motorhome?"

"He said to get it to a storage yard and call him. He'd tell me what to do next."

"What about the GPS tracker you mentioned?"

"Tucker said it had one. He gave me an internet address and password. I logged in and it showed the GPS location of the motorhome. The tracker is probably under the hood, on the driver's side, close to the fuse box."

"Show me."

We walked over to the coach and I popped the hood.

The repo guy looked in the engine compartment and said, "Right there. That little black box."

I nodded. "How do we disable it?"

"Easy. Disconnect the red wire. The box is held on with Velcro. Easy to take off."

I disconnected the wire and pulled the tracker out of the engine bay. There was a flashing red light on the back of it.

I showed it to the repo guy.

"It has a battery backup. Good for about a week."

I thought for a moment then asked, "You driving back to Arkansas?"

"Yep."

"Mind taking this with you? Dropping it into the Mississippi River when you go over the bridge?"

"Yeah, I'll do that."

"Okay. What about the keys Tucker sent you? Let me see them."

He handed me a set of keys. They were copies of the ones I had gotten with the coach. I put them in my pocket.

"One last question. Why'd you stop here? Why not keep going until you were further away?"

The repo guy blew his nose. "After I started driving, my head stopped up; my nose started running; my eyes were watering. I couldn't hardly see or breathe.

"I stopped here to get some fresh air, clear my head, get some tissues and eye drops."

I laughed. "Are you allergic to cats?"

He nodded. "I am. Don't tell me there's a cat in there."

"There is. His name is Mango Bob. He's probably still sleeping on the bed in the back.

"You stay here. I'm going to check and make sure everything inside is okay. If it is, I'm not going to press charges."

Chapter 69

The repo guy followed me to the door. "I promise I wasn't trying to steal it. I didn't take anything out of it. I was just doing my job."

I opened door and stepped into the coach; everything looked untouched. I walked to the back, and, as I expected, Bob was on the bed, sleeping.

Checking the closet and drawers, I saw that nothing was missing.

Satisfied that the repo man hadn't taken anything, I went out and advised the officer I wouldn't be pressing charges. I thanked him for his time, and he left.

I went over to Jack and shook his hand. "Thank you for your help on this. Hope I didn't ruin your afternoon."

He smiled. "No problem. It was fun. It gave me an excuse to get out of the house. Plus I got to meet Sarah. We were talking while you were dealing with the police.

"She seems nice. Told me she dumped you in the water this morning. Bet that was fun."

"Yeah, she's a hoot."

"Walker, you know those two guys you tazed back in Mississippi? The state police picked them up.

"The car they were in was stolen. Both guys had felony warrants. There were two guns in the car. Their phone showed they'd spoken to Tucker the day before they stopped you. He paid them to get the RV.

"Those two won't be getting out on bail. With the gun charges against them, they'll probably do a few years in Mississippi jails. Maybe a stint in Federal prison. You won't have to worry about them or Tucker.

"With him out of the way, I don't think anyone else will be looking for your RV. I think it's over."

I smiled. "That's the best news I've heard all day."

"Walker, I hate to run, but I need to get back home to Jean. I've promised to take her to dinner. I don't want to be late. Sarah says we should get together for dinner next week. She said you'll pay. Jean will be calling to arrange a time."

I laughed. "Jack, at the very least I owe you another dinner. I'll call you later."

He got into his car and drove off.

The repo guy was still there. I asked, "You need a ride?"

"No, my wife's down here with me. I've called and she's heading this way. Even if she weren't coming, I wouldn't get back into that RV. Not after what's happened."

I walked over to Sarah and gave her a hug. "Everything's okay. Bob's safe. Let's go inside and see him."

Chapter 70

After settling everything at Walmart, Sarah drove her truck back to Englewood and I followed in the Love Bus. Bob rode with me.

Driving back was a lot less hectic than the trip over. I was able to relax knowing that Bob was safe and the motorhome was back in my hands.

Hopefully, the Harvey Tucker business was behind me.

Back at Sarah's, I carefully pulled through the gate and parked the RV where it had been before.

When I got out, I made a point of closing and locking the gate.

Sarah had gotten back before me and had already unloaded Bob's food and new litter box into her apartment.

When she saw me locking the gate, she came out and said, "I'll be coming to get Bob in about ten minutes. In the meantime, get your new clothes out of my truck."

She turned and walked back to her apartment. She didn't seem to be in a talkative mood.

I got my new clothes and took them into the motorhome. I'd hang them up later.

Bob was awake. I gave him a few pets and told him that Sarah would soon be taking him home. I told him I'd miss him.

He said, "Murrph."

A few minutes later, Sarah knocked on my door.

When I opened it, she said, "Everything's set up. I'm ready for Bob."

"Okay, I'll get him."

I went to the bedroom and picked him up off the bed. I had planned to carry him to Sarah's place, but she said, "No. I'll carry him from here."

I handed Bob over, and she took him to her apartment, closing the door behind her.

I wasn't invited in.

Chapter 71

I was standing in the boatyard. No invitation by Sarah to come in and join her and Bob, no mention of having dinner together.

Maybe she needed some alone time with her cat.

That was fine with me. There were still two hours of daylight and I had a few things I wanted to do.

First thing on my list was to check the website the repo guy was using to follow the GPS tracker. I wanted to be sure it no longer showed where the Love Bus was parked.

I entered the address and password and looked at the display.

It showed the tracker was on I-75, moving north toward Tampa. Anyone who was monitoring it wouldn't find the Love Bus.

Back inside the coach, I checked the system levels. Battery good, propane good. Black and gray water tanks were almost full. Not good.

With the holding tanks nearly full, it was time to dump them or risk sewage backing up into the shower pan.

Outside, I opened the utility compartment and quickly found the connection to dump the holding tanks. I'd need a sewer hose to connect the motorhome to the pipe in the boatyard.

Checking in the other compartments, I eventually found one. Brown and disgustingly dirty. It looked like someone had splashed sewage on the outside of the hose and hadn't bothered to clean it up.

I remembered what Jack had said about dumping the

tanks. Always wear rubber gloves. I now understood why.

I hadn't remembered to buy a pair and was hoping there might be some in the coach. Maybe under the bathroom sink.

I checked. There were cleaning supplies but no gloves.

As I looked around for other places where they might be stored, I wondered what was under the bed. It looked like the mattress was on a platform. It might lift and there could be storage space underneath.

I checked, and, sure enough, there was a large storage area. But no rubber gloves. Just a metal toolbox. Red, with a chrome handle. It was a long shot, but maybe I'd find gloves in it.

I reached into the space and grabbed the toolbox by the handle and lifted. It didn't budge. Either it was glued to the floor or was a lot heavier than I expected.

On my second try, I planted my feet firmly and grabbed the handle and lifted again. With the extra effort, I was able to get it out. I quickly put it on the floor.

Judging by the weight, I assumed I'd find heavy tools inside. Pipe wrenches, hammers, maybe an anvil.

I unsnapped the two latches and opened the lid. The top shelf did have tools. A set of heavy wrenches. I lifted it out and looked underneath. There were more wrenches. Below them, several white plastic tubes. Ten in all.

I'd seen them before. They were on the GoPro video we'd found. In the briefcase given to Harvey Tucker.

Rolls of gold coins he had been given by the man in the white suit.

Gold was valuable. Each of the coins had to be worth at least a thousand dollars. Maybe a lot more. There were two hundred of them. It might explain why Tucker had been so interested in getting the motorhome back.

He had stashed his gold in it.

Chapter 72

The big question was who did the gold belong to?

It was in my possession. I'd legally purchased the motorhome and presumably everything in it. Including the gold.

Tucker was probably the only person who knew it was there. And he was dead.

If I kept it, no one but me would know.

But I didn't want to keep it and end up in jail if the gold didn't belong to me.

I decided to call Jack.

After three rings, he answered. "Jack, this is Walker. You got a minute?"

"Sure, what's up?"

"First, thanks for your help today. I don't know what I would have done without you."

"No problem. Glad to be of assistance."

"So, Jack, I have a question.

"Let's say that hypothetically I found a gold coin in my motorhome. Probably left there by Tucker.

"If I found one, what should I do with it?"

He thought for a minute then said, "Hypothetically speaking, if you were to find one, I'd say keep it. And don't tell anyone.

"You bought the motorhome and everything in it. That should cover items left by the previous owner. It seems the only person who could claim ownership of the coin would be

Tucker. He's dead and has no relatives. That means there's no one left to make a claim.

"So, I'd say keep it. This is all hypothetical, right?"

"Yeah, it is. I was just wondering what I should do if I stumbled on to one of those coins."

I wasn't sure he was buying the hypothetical part. Especially after he said, "Walker, if it were me, I'd get a safety deposit box at a local bank and put the coin in it. Then, when I needed money, I'd sell it to one of the local coin shops."

I hesitated before I said anything, then, "Yeah, if I were to find a coin or two, I might do that. Put it in a safety deposit box at the bank. I appreciate your advice. Tell Jean I said hello. I'm looking forward to dinner. Thanks again for your help at Walmart. You saved the day."

"Walker, as always, good to talk to you. Let's get together soon."

I ended the call.

Thinking about what Jack had said, the next day might be a good day to visit a local bank.

Chapter 73

With the toolbox and coins safely back under the bed, I carried on with the dirty task of dumping the holding tanks.

It wasn't something I wanted to do, but it had to be done. Either that or no shower and no using the toilet for a while.

After successfully dumping the tanks and cleaning up after, it was well past dinner time.

I had expected to see Sarah. But she hadn't been back out in the yard since getting Bob and had made no mention of eating together when I'd last talked to her.

I called her phone, but she didn't answer. The lights in her apartment were off.

Maybe she had other dinner plans.

My stomach was telling me it was time to eat. Not wanting to leave the motorhome and the thousands in gold under the bed, I took the last TV dinner out of the freezer and heated it in the microwave.

I ate alone. No Bob. No Sarah.

Just me and ten rolls of gold coins no one else knew about.

An hour later, my phone chimed with a call from Molly.

"Hi. Guess you heard about our big adventure today."

"I did, and Sarah's really mad at you!"

"She's mad at me? What'd I do?"

"For starters, you flirted with a senior citizen in a bikini during the training. Then you didn't thank her for taking you clothes shopping. And because of you, someone broke into the boatyard and stole Mango Bob.

"You made her drive across the county chasing down the thief. You almost got yourself killed confronting the guy in the Walmart parking lot.

"Even worse, you didn't offer to take her to dinner after all she did for you!"

"Molly, in my defense, I didn't flirt with the gal in the swimsuit. She was coming on to me. I got away from her as quickly as I could.

"I did thank Sarah for taking me shopping. I even bought her lunch.

"And I did recover Bob. No one got hurt.

"I would have asked her to dinner, but she took Bob and left without inviting me over. She didn't answer when I called.

"So I ate alone. I don't know what else I could have done."

Molly grunted, then said, "Walker, you have a lot to learn about women.

"After a day like today, Sarah needed someone to talk to. It should have been you. You should have knocked on her door, asked her to dinner and treated her nicely after the rough day she's had."

She was right.

"Molly, I messed up. I should have done all those things. So is it too late? Should I call her now, see if she wants to eat?"

"No, it's too late. She ate alone. Just her and Bob.

"But you'll get another chance tomorrow. Start by being nice to her. Don't flirt with other women. Ask her to dinner.

"You're camping in her backyard. You're a part of her life now. So be nice."

"Molly, I promise I'll do better."

"Good. Now tell me what the repo guy told you about Tucker."

I told her the story, leaving out the part about the gold coins.

"Well, it sounds like you guys had a busy day. I can see why Sarah might be upset. You could have gotten hurt."

"Molly, don't worry. It ended well. We got Bob and the motorhome back.

"I'm sorry about upsetting Sarah. I'll try to smooth things over tomorrow."

We said our goodbyes and ended the call.

Chapter 74

I didn't sleep much that night. Thinking about the events of the day. The coins, Sarah, Bob.

My phone chimed me awake at six thirty. Sarah's lights weren't on. She was still sleeping.

I dressed and slipped out the gate, making sure to lock it behind me. I headed down Dearborn toward the corner market.

I wanted to pick up some supplies and get a local paper, to see if we made the news.

Unlike the previous morning, Dearborn was packed with cars. All heading toward the market.

A news truck with a satellite dish was parked in the street. A long line of people waited to get into the store.

As I got closer, a young man walking my way asked, "Are you the one?"

"What do you mean?"

He smiled. "Didn't you hear? The winning ticket from last night's Florida lottery was sold here yesterday morning. Someone won nine million dollars!"

I had given the tickets to Sarah. Maybe she had the winning one.

I turned and walked back to her place. Her lights were still off. It didn't matter. I was going to wake her.

I knocked on her door. She didn't answer. I knocked louder. Her lights came on.

A few moments later, she opened the door a few inches. "What?"

She was wearing a long T-shirt, nothing else.

She asked again, "What?"

I smiled. "Get dressed; I've got something to show you. You're going to love it."

"No, it's too early. Leave me alone."

"Sarah, listen to me. There's something you need to see. Get dressed and let me show you. Today might be your lucky day."

And it was.

The adventure continues...

Follow the further adventures of Mango Bob, John Walker and Sarah Burke at: www.mangobob.com

Other books in the Mango Bob series include:

Mango Lucky

Mango Bay

Mango Glades

Mango Key

Mango Blues

Mango Digger

Mango Crush

Mango Motel

Mango Star

Mango Road

You can find photos, maps, and more from the Mango Bob adventures at http://www.mangobob.com

Stay in touch with Mango Bob and Walker on Facebook at: www.facebook.com/MangoBob

Thanks for reading!

Made in the USA
Monee, IL
27 April 2021

67033507R00184